The *Golden* Rings

The *Golden* Rings

The Spell of the Golden Rings Guides the Destiny of the Twin Flames

Prequel to 'Twin Flame Reunion'

by

Coral Y. Cross

Disclaimer: Although this story is a novel/paranormal romance based on facts, aside from the twin flames (whose characters do exist) any other characters in this book are entirely fictional and any resemblance to those living or dead is co-incidental.

This book can be identified as the Prequel to another book by this author: Twin Flame Reunion already published on Amazon in 2021. They are part of The Twin Flame Saga and the third book called 'Destiny of the Twin Flames' is the third in the saga.

Cover Design Concept: Coral Y. Cross. Cover Designer Aila Design
Cover Meaning: *The actual original true two rings are joined together and the inside inscription can be seen. Representing the destiny guided lives of Angel and Knight. This artwork contains one of the original Golden Rings.*

*This book is dedicated
to the magic of Destiny in our
lives*

For Bruce

...

My Eternal Twin Flame

~ CONTENTS ~

PART THREE: **The Love & Passion**

*After the storm and
after the rain*

...

You are still my Flame

Wherever you go

...

I will be with you

PROLOGUE

I am the narrator of this book and also a character. "So Knight: You may know exactly what I'm going to say here. That from my point of view the Twin Flame incarnation is well understood. I fully know now that I am part of this destiny with you. Our soul is One but split between two people."

The Golden Rings feature to connect us even further. These rings are in existence for the purpose of this current incarnation connection and will always bring us back together because they cannot be disintegrated ever. Gold can be melted but cannot disappear.

Pure gold is virtually indestructible. It will not corrode, rust or tarnish, and cannot be destroyed by fire. While the rings are not pure gold but are 18ct, which is 75% gold. Pure gold would be too soft for wearing and would damage easier. The Jeweller chose 18ct for the rings. So far, in 55 years they have endured one being lost in the depths of water and the other not worn again until recently.

Pre 1946: The Rings were chosen with care, as was the Jeweller. The incantations before they were made and the spiritual guides' choices for the Inscriptions caused everything to fall into place in our world. At all times Cause and Effect are in play here as is the case in every event, in all incarnations and all paths on Earth.

From the very first time back in 1968 when we, the chosen ones, the Twin Flames, purchased 'The Rings' and even before that, back to eons before 1946, these rings held magic and our destiny was guided from within their energy. Their energy was a spell and an incantation spoken and decreed by our spirit guides and our One Soul. This was during our visit to Dimension 7 before our birth.

The Rings spoke to us, the Twin Flames, and we responded by purchasing them and bringing their magic into our love affair of this incarnation together. Who could have known the full magic and power they possessed? No-one did at that time on Earth. Our power can even reach far and beyond this lifetime we are living together. We will remain together in our travels throughout infinity.

We are incredibly fortunate in that we were guided to choose the exact right star signs to be born under. The two signs are the most matched in passion and love — Scorpio and Pisces. Check this out and search it if you wish, but you will find the answer is always Scorpio and Pisces the best and highest match in the entire zodiac. This choosing completes us and brings us the joy in this lifetime of living through a Twin Flame existence and finding the most passionate and rewarding love of all.

This Love Story echoes back into the past and connects to the entire universe on every level and dimension overseen by the 'Supreme Being' who created everything, including us. It is my story but it includes my Twin Flame and that makes us One. Therefore it is Our story.

"So I can talk to you, Knight, and you can listen if you are awakened. If this is the case, then you will change your mind. You will run back home to me. This will be our completion."

"And I, Angel, will be waiting."

The parts where Angel speaks her own story are marked with the heading of – Angel –

*We need to recognise the pact
and ever lasting love …*

That our love was always there

It never left …

We just had to see it

PART ONE:

The Creation of Destinies

To Love Truly

...

Is To Love

Without Boundaries

CHAPTER 1

Knight: 1946

*I*n the Beginning his tiny body that is one half of this soul is growing and starting life inside the womb. He has already chosen his mother long ago. It is 1946 and he is birthed at the time arranged by the stars and the universal field. The stars are guiding the planets, moons, Earth and the entire solar system. They are all in alignment. This is his moment.

His view of the world comes from that light-filled explosion of birth. This soul looks forward to his childhood and then the meeting with his Twin Flame.

And his name shall be: Knight

Of course, his name is also pre-ordained. He awaits his twin flame's birth the following year. She, his eternal Twin Flame, will also explode into humanity. Their stars match up for passion and power. He is a Scorpio (fire and passion) and she a Pisces (softness and love). Each has what the other seeks. Those birthdays match up with the plans of the stars for both of them. This is the beginning of a typical Twin Flame birth connection. All is pre-destined and pre-ordained. In their future lives on Earth they will be constantly guided and pulled towards their destinies. For many years in their early lives, they may not feel this guidance but all the same it still gets them to where they should be at any given time and place. For the success of this twin flame incarnation they will both be required to 'awaken' later in life before they pass on from this Earth life.

He starts his life surrounded by the angels, growing up with a family with two siblings. These siblings have their own karmic lifetimes to fulfil. They will, all the same, nudge his direction many times. This will often look like they are causing him harm or stress but this also guides people on to their real tasks.

As he travels through his childhood, all is well and he is content. He does well at his schooling and forges through into high school levels. Here he concentrates his energies on commercial studies. His future now is sealed for his career and success in life. He will always be successful.

After school he goes to work with his father for a company in the office. This is not his career yet but he will soon move on from this. He is working here at this company so that he can come into contact with his twin flame's father at work.

This is first contact.

The Parents' Meeting

No-one knows at this stage. The fathers are friends — one being a worker and the other being the manager. At some point here something stressful occurs. Someone in the company steals at work but the father of the female Twin Flame is blamed, for some unknown star guided reason. It creates a bad feeling between these two men. One loses his job over this incident. The manager knows it was not this man who stole. As all this goes on behind the scenes and the Twin Flames have no idea. They still apparently do not even know each other yet.

Their energies are matching but not the same. They come from the same source, the same soul. But they are not the same because half is the female energy and the other half is the male energy. Every soul has female and male energy within them because there is no such thing as a female or male soul. This only occurs in human physical life here on Earth for reasons of evolvement also.

Therefore those different aspects from the One soul will show up differently in individual aspects of the joined couple. They will therefore not appear as twins with one mind which is why the 'break' can and will occur and also it is destined.

She will have the soft loving features of the female Pisces energy and he will have the power and passion of the male energy from this One Soul. He, throughout his life, will always seek her and her energy and she will forever seek him. No matter what appears to go wrong. It is forever destined and their star signs work for them throughout life.

All this time the rings are waiting. Waiting and waiting … The rings are an all important play in the game. The gold sits waiting also as the rings have not been made yet. They start to be made after the Twin Flames meet and spend their time together in a romantic magical era on Earth.

It was always part of the plan that the rings were to be made in the 1960s to match the couple's life and sit waiting for them to arrive at that specific jewellery shop where they sit in a cabinet both together and matching, their spell smouldering. Only those who know about the spell and pact would be aware of this energy.

The Rings will sit and wait in the jewellery shop until these souls are pulled in their direction to purchase them for a lifetime of connection. The energies in the gold of the rings will pull them together forevermore. The Rings that sit and wait for many years and seem dormant, are, all that time, creating the build-up of energies that will guarantee to keep them together and always return them to each other. The message inside the rings will reverberate throughout the entire universe. The words are now written on the universal field forever and their meaning is a burning script. Other souls will take notice and learn from The Rings.

The Guardianship of the Rings

The spiritual guides represent the guardianship of not only the Golden Rings but the One Soul couple — the lovers.

They will follow and guide them all throughout their current Twin Flame lifetime. It matters not if they get separated or stay together. They will endure.

They are Twin Flames and that is very different to soul mates. Soul mates are anybody and everyone you meet in a lifetime and they leave a mark on your life and help steer your path. Anyone at all who participates in a life lesson for you. It can be your romantic partner or even an enemy. As long as they push your buttons and create change in you then they are your soul mates.

They must always remember that The Rings play a huge role in this relationship. These rings guide and steer their destiny. These two gold rings signify they are part of a sacred relationship. For many people their rings start off being all important but then later they are discarded and mean nothing. In those cases the rings have no part to play in their energies.

These particular Rings have been given life to participate in the play. Angel and Knight know this. As long as even one ring remains in the physical possession of even one Twin Flame then the energy remains and even connects to any situation of any lost ring. The lost ring is also still alive!

It is Angel, who secretly kept possession of one ring. It is her ring. It has travelled to five different places she has lived in over many years. It has never been lost and remained in a small velvet bag with a string tied at the top. No matter what happened to her or around her over those years it remained in Angel's possession. Somehow she just knew it had a life of its own. She could never disconnect from it.

Miraculously she still has it, because Angel has never been good at storing and keeping things. It stayed close to her like a magnet. It looked at her and it waited for her. It waited for her to action all the built-up emotions and connections that remained within both of them all along.

She often thought to herself, "I took out that velvet bag and handled and looked at the rings. I did this many, many times. Yes, two rings, as there was also the gold and diamond ring (engagement)."

The appearance of pain and suffering and the breaking of the relationship had been set as their destiny from the start. They don't realise that they can eliminate pain and suffering at any time if they choose not to see it. Knight needs to learn this.

They don't need to look back and blame anyone or even themselves for situations that arose to cause separation and pain. It is always as it should be. It was all needed. The reasons and the experience of the healing and the joy with reunion are all in the destiny the Twin Flames first chose.

Angel has waited far too long it seems. It looks that way. "Will he now awaken and return?" she ponders constantly. She begins to wonder but holds steady to her faith in the spell and their destiny together. She knows it will be as he said it would be.

They simply must remember always, the path that contains pain and suffering is the learning, and the reunion is the reward. They met again recently at a family event. She sat near him and secretly flashed 'the' golden ring she was wearing towards him. She mentally sent the spell's golden particles to him — to his heart — to his mind. Then wrapped them all around both of them. So this is the insight into who Knight is and how the rings fit into everything.

It matters not that in the future they are both now growing older everyday and they may imagine it is getting too late. But thankfully they have the spell on them and the sacred pact — so they cannot ever waiver. It is their power and their strength as well as their guiding light.

This spell will make sure everything works as it should. There is a powerful guardian to this pact and spell. That means reunion can't fail ever.

It now depends on Knight waking up.

Wake Up Knight!

~~~

Run To Me

When You Need Me So

...

Run To Me

I can't let you go

...

CHAPTER 2

Knight: The Scorpio Sign

*S*corpio is the sign that has three symbols: the Scorpion, the Eagle, and the Phoenix. His colours are red, scarlet and rust. Knight is a water sign, as is Angel the Pisces fish sign. He is resourceful, brave, powerful and passionate. He is assertive and has strong determination and focus. He will always seek the truth behind anything important. He is dedicated and fierce. The perfect sign for a Twin Flame half who needs all these traits to bring home his love for the reuniting.

Dear Knight:
Your Pisces Twin Flame (Angel) is the perfect match to give you all you desire and more. No other zodiac sign will match you more. This match between Scorpio and Pisces is one of the most intense in the zodiac.

They both match on the physical and emotional level and take their physical attraction extremely seriously. On the sexual level they are highly compatible and both match with an intense desire to possess the other totally.

Scorpio is ruled by two planets. Only five of the zodiac signs are ruled by two planets. Mars is the ancient ruler and Pluto is the modern ruler. Mars represents his driving ambition while Pluto represents his deep mysterious forces.

Scorpio's erogenous zones are genitals, eyes and neck. They are highly sexual and their eyes possess a major attraction. They love eye contact.

When these two signs are matched, both need to be aware that this is a perfect match and you need to grab this relationship with both hands and never let go. The physical connection can be so electrical that it sends both partners (Scorpio and Pisces) to the heights of ecstasy.

Angel has always recognised who her Knight is in the zodiac because he represents all that she desires.

This is where their match will be so intense that it flows over into the paranormal romance. There will be fireworks, lightning, full-on tornadoes and passionate connections. They are very emotionally compatible. Both being water signs they will be emotionally sensitive to each other. Scorpio has passionate desires.

The actual three stages of Scorpio denote his transformation that leads to the Reunion. When he has completed the three stages then they are One again. Scorpio also has the numbers 666 and 777 as luck and good fortune and these numbers match to Pisces. Of course, this was all intentionally designed for them. Their matching and their destiny of the reunion will bring about the healing of an entire extended family. All hearts will be repaired by all they agreed to, eons before 1946 and 1947.

3 Stages:
1) The Scorpion — stings, self protection
2) The Eagle — evolving and ambitious
3) The Phoenix — transforming into the light

The Phoenix represents rising from its own ashes.

Therefore Knight, as a powerful Scorpio, must reach the Stage of number 3 — The Phoenix — before he can awaken and rejoin his love. Angel's energies are continuing to daily awaken him and stir his heart back to where they both were when they agreed to their pact and plan.

Knight's very intense Scorpio energy can hold him back many times. Scorpio has a strong stubborn streak that is hard to get beyond. Fortunately in Knight's case, his heart can soften eventually, sometimes very quickly. In other words, he can be convinced by the right person.

His stubbornness would be fighting and defending him against the fact that she left him. He has to get to understand that it was not just her decision and that all the illusions are now seen for the truth of what they are. She was forced all along by the spell and he had done nothing in those last few years together to show her he loved her deeply still. She had been waiting 6 long years for him.

He had been in Stage 1 far too long and also must emerge from Stage 2 right now. The year 2023 (7) says that he is ready and will reunite in the most passionate love he has ever been exposed to. Because Angel, being soft but naive, kept her tremendous passions to herself previously instead of unleashing them as she will now when the reunion releases all.

Scorpio is a very devoted sign. Knight has given away his secrets to her more than once. Angel now knows he is ripe to awaken and return to her.

On three occasions at least he has divulged that Angel is the love of his life. Even after meeting his current partner and at a party for their 'engagement'. Knight: You have also told her directly you 'hate' her current partner. If this anger still runs deep in your heart it's because you still and always will, love Angel.

She will love and heal your heart so that hate can never enter and harm you again. Her greatest desire is to mend you and watch over you, making sure you both live your lives to the fullest this time. She will always protect you, as you will protect her.

~~~

You Will Love Me,

Always and Ever

...

That Message is Understood

The Golden Rings

CHAPTER 3

Angel: 1947

The Next Beginning is the second tiny body that is the other half of this soul who was also growing and starting life inside the womb. The true magic here is that they were in the womb at the same time for 4 months before his birth. They would definitely have communicated while in the womb. Both sets of parents did not live very far from each other all this time. They still had not met. That was to be when one father started working with the other and then an incident occurred there to bring about a kind of sadness and resentment within her family. Of course the Twin Flames knew nothing about this at the time.

She also has been birthed now, at the time arranged by the stars and the universal field. Everything to do with the planets, moons and the entire Earth's solar system is still in place since his birth to encircle also her birth.

The right planetary time, day and month

And her name shall be: Angel

Her name is also pre-ordained. Now that she is also peering out with wonderment for the life they will lead together.

They are instantly joined in the physical world now. Their auras are matching. They still have not 'met' but are joined here on Earth, Now.

Two newborns have now started on their journey even though, as humans, they have no real idea yet. This can't happen until their meeting when they have grown and matured to the right time. This place has been made sacred. It seems ordinary but it is not.

North Road, Oakleigh 1963

That place will be when she is 16 and he has just turned 17. Still children really. That is why it will always and ever be innocent and beautiful. Man can damage it, change it, rebuild it and even move the road where they first met but the co-ordinates will remain the same forever.

It now also takes 'The Golden Rings' and 'The Jeweller' to join in with these two Flames on their life journey. They are all now connected with the sacred vows and spells. Her life from that meeting onwards changed dramatically.

For her, as that Earth person and being very young still, she then may or may not have noticed huge changes when they met but they were glaring out at both of them. She hadn't really noticed she was alone but she certainly noticed now that she wasn't. She had a full life before that time with her friends, dancing, music, swimming, bike riding, travelling to the city and trampolining competitions.

But right from the start of their meeting he filled her life with all that she had ever desired. That kind of love was so new to her. He seemed to know from the start not to overpower her. They were both similar in that way, in that they allowed their relationship and love to progress at its own pace. She had previously had a quite few males interested in her — even pursuing her. But they had never held her interest for very long. She never connected to any of them. They were simply not The One. She knew instantly when 'He' turned up that day.

Her days were spent without any kind of worry or trouble. The nights they often went to the many venues where there were well known live bands and dancing. Sometimes movies but dancing was their favourite. He fitted in well with her family and became very quickly like an extra son to her parents.

Angel, being a Pisces, also is very much over-sensitive when it comes to love and emotions. Therefore she cannot tolerate living in a relationship where there is no love. She made a huge mistake when she originally left Knight behind because she was only under an illusion that he had stopped loving her. He made it clear at the time of the split that he did love her but she found it almost impossible back then to go against the force of the spell. This mistake was, of course, always planned.

In her current relationship — she wishes to leave even more urgently because she is aware daily that this partner does not love her. He has a neurological condition whereby he can't show love or intimacy. She is devastated to be in this empty relationship. It started in what appeared to be new love and changes but soon failed to be fulfilling for her. She was asleep then. She is awake now and has also been turned back to the truth by the spell of their Twin Flame pact.

Because she is awake she is aware that this second marriage and poor relationship had to occur.

Angel gets more and more agitated and depressed because of the waiting game. Her lack of sleep is harming her heart further. She has a lot to do to bring about the perfect circumstances for the reunion and new connection. But the closer it gets the more anxious she gets.

She realises she must stop to make time to show and feel her gratefulness and the feeling of imminent joy in her life. Keeping to that practice and also meditating certainly interrupts the depression and helps with the faith for the manifesting.

But … There's a huge hole in her heart …

– Angel –

Bruce you were always and forever my only true love. *My other half. My flame of passion.* I don't know why (except of course for the spell and pact that forced us) but we drifted away from each other as we went through the trials of life, births and problems. It didn't have to be. Except it actually did have to be. At various times we both went through depression and anxiety and spent lonely times apart when we should always have joined together.

But I now know we both learnt from our mistakes. That is the purpose of them in life. Therefore we will be together again with everything sad wiped away for good. No tears ever again. Every life pain rolls off our shoulders together now.

The Standout Memories: Those moments of my life are from way before I met 'the other ogre'. They start from that spring/summer of 1963. The start of our lives in this lifetime. We seemed oblivious to the rest of the world. Knight brushing my long hair, washing my hair, his hand, his touch, his beauty. Things we did and places we went. These are all filled with magic feelings. But the magic feelings don't really come from the places but from you, Knight.

I love you more than I can say and as much as I can show and do and it's only me for you. I'm not afraid to start again even though it takes huge courage. I swear I am making my way back to you.

"I will reach you and you can reach me. We will meet running towards each other and we will plan from then on our entire future that is our destiny and throughout all of infinity. Amen," I whisper to Knight and the entire universe. The universal angels and guides listen. They act. They help us manifest our love desires on Earth.

We will be joining forever — the wedding, family party, a new house suitable for us both together and a car that's ours alone. This new house will welcome all of our family. Our own families — not other people's that just don't fit it. It is our blood only now.

"Knight, hear my heart beat next to yours. It's not the kind of love you've ever felt or known before or after. It's our love and it's special and can't be broken apart," I softly speak directly to you Knight. It started off so innocent and naive. We had so much to learn and were given this opportunity to learn in this lifetime — the One Soul split into two incarnations. This love would suddenly burst into life, it would wane for a while, it would split for too long — but then it would rejoin and burst with the highest passion and flames. This burning love never to be known again by anyone but us two.

We were once so young. Our hearts were strong and healthy. Never realising one day they would both break and cry for a very long time. That is the frailty of innocence — never knowing what is to come. But once souls start on a journey like this they must also become brave.

How can I, Angel, forget you or any part of you? I was actually born to love you and you only. I can never be free of that loving hold. You will always and ever be a part of me and I of you. Nothing can stop us now.

Absolutely everything reminds me of you. No matter where I go or what I do. I feel you always! If I catch your scent I am instantly transported away.

I've never known love like ours and neither have you. Knowing you're with me now and forever makes everything ok. You've no idea how much I love you do you? I always have and always will.
Now, maybe you do know!
Why? Because I have now found the courage to tell you everything that matters to both of us.

So, come right back. I can hardly bear it now because I've got so much love for you. Let us share it and tell the world.

Because …

The world vibrates when our eyes meet. So I await that moment when our eyes meet again and we feel those vibrations to the depths of our very One Soul.

~~~

It's the same love

It's the same hearts

...

That we were at the start

CHAPTER 4

Angel: The Pisces Sign

isces is emotionally sensitive, gracious and intensely aware. The star sign Pisces is regarded as the most sympathetic of all the signs in the zodiac. They will go to any lengths to ensure the happiness of those around them. They are also imaginative and creative.

Dear Angel: Pisces is most attracted to Scorpio. There's no surprise there. Their will can be swayed by others as they hate confrontation or hurting people. They become easily hurt and often withdraw rather than stand up for themselves. Pisces people have supernatural intuition. This allows them to know other people's intentions and to seek out messages from the universe.

When it comes to love and physical connection Pisces are turned on by touch. Anything at all like hair brushing, massage, kissing, touching the skin, massaging feet, touching anywhere secret like in the folds of the neck.

When touched they are melting into your energy. Pisces is the zodiac's romantic dreamer. Their erogenous zones are the feet, toes, hands and head. They love soft touch and sweet words.

Pisces is another zodiac sign that has two rulers. Jupiter is their ancient ruler and Neptune is the modern ruling planet. Jupiter rules for gifts, luck, tolerance and spiritual growth. While Neptune rules dreams, psychic ability, illusion and deception. Mystical Neptune and Jupiter combine to make Pisces sweet and sensitive. This is what makes Pisces dreamy and sensitive because Neptune and Jupiter are known to be highly spiritual planets.

Pisces eyes are particularly dreamy appearing that they are always looking off to far distant places. Their main weakness is always putting others before themselves. The Pisces power is linked to their ruler Neptune, the planet of spirituality. They are the empaths of the cosmos and they are profoundly intuitive and psychic. Their number is 777 which is the universal number of luck.

Having, as already said, their zodiac signs chosen before birth, it goes without saying as to why Scorpio and Pisces were chosen for them to be born under. Amongst the entire zodiac these two signs reign as the most advantageous for connecting and being love partners.

When love is involved, particularly romantic love, Scorpio and Pisces are two signs that become intense, right away and very quickly. They are both deep emotional Water Signs who were born to seek out their soulmate/twin flame.

These two signs in particular, burn for each other. The element of water is naturally connected with feeling. Scorpio is associated with merging on the most intimate level and Pisces with the subterranean energy of mystical infusion. They both long for each other and will never stop seeking.

Angel and Knight have been gifted to be born under these zodiac signs so that they have, while on Earth, a paranormal rapport. Water signs tend to follow their heart. When they sense this in the other, they tend not to pause but to jump in immediately.

This is exactly how it was when they met. They sensed their never ending connection from the start. So immediately there was union.

Scorpio and Pisces signs trine each other. In astrology this means they form a 120 degree angle to one another. This equates to bringing each other harmony, luck, expansiveness and joy. Therefore there is a physical and paranormal attraction and connection to one another. Trines are a most favourable aspect to share with another sign and means a trio of signs that has a connecting thread between them.

They both have a karmic fortunate connection to each other coming from a past life.

Both Scorpio and Pisces have something that no other two signs will ever have. They have sexual and emotional release through their love making. This also means that no matter what trials their journey takes them on, they will always view their relationship as super special in the universe. Their connection is almost telepathic and they can easily 'know' what each other is thinking and feeling at anytime when they need support.

Scorpio is the most potent and Pisces is the most imaginative. This combination is the fire that is fulfilling for both of them. The combination of wild passion and soft inner sensing, also of fires burning and the capture and release of searing energies. They attract to each other like magnets.

When it comes to Angel and Knight their budding connection at such a young age meant for this lifetime that they remained innocent and reticent. Their fire and passions of ecstasy were not released to their full potential early on. This was intentional so as to bring about the heightened fire and passions that they would release later in life after their reunion.

Scorpio is a fixed water sign that can be intense and overbearing and may verge on jealousy or fear of betrayal. Pisces is a mutable water sign that is softer and more tender. Pisces can find intense love with Scorpio and Scorpio can give Pisces the attention they crave. They are matched beyond measure in the whole of the human zodiac world.

The sexually submissive Pisces is the perfect match for Scorpio's dominant and raw sexual energy. They both receive what they are seeking. Only the unique powers of Pisces can truly understand the complicated emotions of the Scorpio. Their sexual chemistry is unmatched.

The whole reason behind the choice of pearls by Angel for their wedding both times coincides with the connection of Pisces and Scorpio to pearls. Pearls are from the ocean and these two signs are water signs.

The bride wore a pearl necklace, a gift from her parents, at their first wedding and she will be wearing the exact same necklace plus pearl stud ear-rings at their second wedding and that choice helps seal them for eternity.

~~~

The Golden Rings

Scorpio

Pisces

Both water signs
Water signs are the most emotional

The words we spoke

The actions we took

...

They are all in alignment

with Destiny

CHAPTER 5

The Meeting: 1963
– Angel –

*T*his is the day I met my love. Life began right then and there. We were oblivious to the whirlpool we had just entered. We were not developed enough in the ways of the world, love or anything really then. We were as naive as you could be in the 1960s. No matter — that was, in fact, our very beauty that made us shine in a crowd.

We flowed and matched together quickly and naturally. Everything we did together from that day on was memorable and filled with joy. Even those so many moments we simply accepted without treasuring the memories — well, they come back to us now and we not only remember but that memory energy that comes forward in time and catches up with us makes its mark on our mind, body and soul. It shows us the joy we seemed to have left behind.

The actual meeting, although of course planned by the pact, seemed very accidental. My friend and I were waiting for a bus on a main road after our night class one evening. A car came along and she knew the driver from her job. They asked to pick us up and we got in the car. I got in the back of the car and 'my dearest love of all time' was also sitting in the back seat. He was the driver's brother. I can't recall all the details but we looked at each other and that was the beginning of something huge for us.

It looks like we didn't even notice but it all catches up now because of the spell. The spell makes sure that nothing is lost. Our lives in entirety are kept behind a secret door and the spell has the key.

That is the day I met my love — with the laughing eyes, the beautiful hair and zest for life. He loved life and he loved me and I returned all of that to him. I'm pretty sure we were very misunderstood by those around us but we did not care. They should all just let us be.

If I had not had that connection to a love of the practice of typing (yes, on a typewriter then) the opportunity to meet at those co-ordinates would seem not to have occurred. But, because of the before life spell and pact and also because we are given very effective powers in our lifetimes, it would still have occurred some other way.

We are not always made aware of our powers in life on Earth so sometimes we can create life situations we do not intend to. Such as, when I perceived myself to be unhappy and unloved in midlife with Knight, my mis-directed power directed me to meet someone else and run away. Now that I am 'awake' I would never create that. We can very easily be fooled when under any kind of powerful spell.

I did not know I was using a powerful energy when going through this part of my life. I was inexperienced and unknowledgeable in the use of my spiritual powers. This power I had been gifted increased as I matured.

It actually kind of got out of control as is the case with most unawakened humans in their lifetimes.

That is why, when you are pondering on life situations, always use your mind to create the most positive outcome for yourself. If you dwell on the negative things right in front of you and even fear or expect things to get worse — then they most definitely will.

Your mind can take you on a journey to wherever you direct it to. This is the Secret to Manifesting that not many understand.

~~~

The Golden Rings

CHAPTER 6

Innocence: 1968

*T*heir *wedding day had arrived.* It was November 1968 on a Saturday afternoon. It was such a beautiful day. The sun shone. They were surrounded by love and family and many soul mates here for their journey to start.

Everything went to plan. The white dress, the lace and the tulle. The white taxi and her Dad on her arm. Their family was all around them. They never gave a thought to the fact that they were innocents. They sped through that day finishing up with Angel dressed in pink linen. A mini dress and matching coat. It was the fashion of that era. Her outfit was made by a dressmaker.

Her love played the song 'Beautiful, beautiful brown eyes'. Knight had organised it with the band to surprise her when she arrived in the pink outfit ready to leave with him. In their minds they would drive away in their iconic green FJ Holden and be happy ever after. There was not a worry at all.

Abbeygate Street, Oakleigh – 30/11/1968

Most significant of all was the ceremony and the fact that they now wore The Golden Rings. The inside inscription burned into their skin. It was telling them something. Did they actually know and feel this at that time? They seemed unaware. But somehow Angel felt from the first idea planted in her head for that inscription that it meant far more than anyone else could tell.

All the same, it was a stunning omission that they had actually never been together in physical union. Neither of them had even looked into those facts or sought advice. Of course, for innocents, they would absolutely not give this a thought.

They were both pure white virgins at their marriage. This had advantages and disadvantages. There could now be regrets on both sides but this worked well for their life story. After all it never even crossed their minds anything was missing.

They were happy with it all but perhaps the delay in their physical love completion was a causative factor to holding back on the powerful passions trapped inside them. They are now due to explode out and be acted on. The gifts due for their troubles.

Their first night together loomed. Still they were not worried or nervous. Knight had booked everything in advance. They stopped first at a hotel/ motel kind of place. Upstairs in their booked room she went to open her suitcase so she could have a shower. "Oh, no!" she exclaimed. Her suitcase is locked and the key is missing. She omitted to bring it. This could spoil the entire honeymoon.

Everything else had gone to plan all day. Not to worry. Knight always had answers and took charge of events. He was truly her protector – The Scorpio. Angel on the other hand, was the Pisces – soft, loving and never having had to make all the decisions even at home with her parents, who had always also been her protectors.

He rang her Dad, who drove to them and brought the key. It might have been so embarrassing. By the time Knight got back into the rooms — she was in the shower. Their memories would blur here. But when it came to their physical connection she does remember they were both a bit unsure. When innocents come face to face with their next step in life — all knowledge that they do not have — it tends to be pushed into the background.

– Angel – We attempted union. We were naive, innocent and completely unknowledgeable. We had never even thought to educate ourselves. It was not done back then. You either found out everything from others or from your inept behaviours of trying out or you knew nothing on your wedding night.

— We slept —

We left in the morning for our forest retreat for our honeymoon. Knight had found the right place for us. He organised all of it. It was beautiful.

It would not be for many years that I, Angel, regretted that we spent 5 years together without allowing all the passion to consume us. I need to accept that this situation was the making of the Twin Flames and the spell all along.

We now have forever to make up for that. We also have a second honeymoon to go to that goes to plan. It's going to be an amazing plan and we will go together where neither of us has been with anyone else before.

It was all part of the spell and the pact. It worked for our current life story. We both must accept this to move on to further heights.

~~~

Where was I ?

Where were You ?

When we went through
our trials in Life

CHAPTER 7

The Rings: Pre 1946

*T*he Rings came into existence long before the birth of the Twin Flames. As did their joining and swearing to the pact before their incarnation here on Earth. They have matching souls of their own.

The Grand Lord of Twin Flames decreed the rings to exist and his workers in the spirit dimension formed how they would look and feel. At that time the rings were connected energetically to Angel and Knight. This meant they could never choose any other rings and that the time and space for the choosing could not be altered.

From 1963 to 1968 they never even thought about what rings they would choose. They did not need to even think about this. They did not know, of course, but the choosing had been done for them.

As has been done since time began, their spiritual paths had been forged out ahead of 'time'. Everyone has a path to follow but not everyone awakens to their path in life. Many have to wait for later lifetimes to fulfil their true destiny. Many humans find it hard to awaken at all while on Earth. This planet of humans is extremely chaotic and confusing for most who incarnate here.

For the Twin Flames their path is to be eternally connected with swirling energies of love and light from before their births. Then on their path they go through many challenges both physically and emotionally.

They somehow lose sight of each other and their love after enduring these deep dark challenges. It appears that their love is stretched to the limit and that it then 'breaks'. But this is all illusion on the surface. Underneath all this they can never ever be parted. Their love cannot be broken.

Their full path consists of far more than that. They will go through the darkness, fight for their survival, and eventually find their own kind of peace. But the peace they find is not their destiny. Their destiny is still each other and their reunion that mends many people and also complete families. Their spiritual work is for many not just themselves.

The Rings are very patient for many years. The Rings are vital to the complete story and Earth path. The ring that ends up at the bottom of a lake waits too, knowing that its job is still being done. First Angel, then Knight will awaken to the guidance from even this lost ring. It is only lost by intentional purpose. It remains visible to all in the spiritual dimension.

Let us not forget also about the inscription that will be engraved inside each ring. This also has been decreed before they were birthed. That was pre 1946.

It was an inspired inscription that opened up inside Angel's mind after they purchased the rings. She had no idea where that thought came from. She just went ahead and had the inscriptions done. She did have a small awakening at that time because she felt something open up within her heart and soul when they had been engraved.

~~~

When choosing your path

Be Brave

...

Take Action

But Never Fear

...

CHAPTER 8

The Rings: 1967

*T*he Rings Observe life from where they wait. They watch the entire interaction between the sacred couple. From the day they met, when angels sang and the stars steered everything into place, and until the theory of everything comes into play. All of their meetings and their acting of the parts they are in the play of life.

They wait! They watch! The rings are patient as they know already when they will be purchased and touched by these angel Twin Flames.

The sacred couple's life is mapped out by destiny before them. They know nothing of the trials and separations that will plague them. These trials come to them for their evolvement and learning because they currently are innocents and extremely naive.

They must learn and learn well. They sit and hug together with no thoughts of the pains ahead of them. These two rings take their part in this universal story very seriously. They are, after all, central to this play on the Earth plane.

For years the couple have no idea how important The Golden Rings are. The rings will stay with them until 1980 when they will be split and separated. One will be lost. No-one could have foreseen this event, least of all the Twin Flame couple. It came out of nowhere.

The Rings have always had a life and soul of their own. They have agreed to participate in this lifetime destiny agreement with the One Soul who has split in two to incarnate as a female and a male human. Their part in this is to solidify the Twin Flames' act of joining forevermore. They watch, they wait, they also give off golden energy especially once the lovers have put these rings on in the church. This is when the magic clicks into place. All of this occurs at that very moment in the beautiful family church.

The Rings have always known that they will at some point be parted, as will the Twin Flames.

As the Twin Flames will be reunited at a certain date and time on Earth, also so will the Rings bring about the reuniting. The lost Ring will not be found. Simply getting back the lost Ring will mean they are stuck in the old energies. The very act, in the future, of the couple reuniting and seeking out to buy a new matching Golden Ring is all about the healing and mending of hearts. This act they participate in will send out vibes to the universal field showing the universe they have understood and participated in the Sacred Pact.

The original Golden Ring will stay lying at the bottom of the lake and the new Ring signifies new life, rekindled love and forgiveness. It will still watch how love and life plays out for the Twin Flames and send its energy to the new Ring. If they had replaced the Golden Ring at the time it was lost then it would not have had the true meaning of connection because the replacement would not have been for the sake of the Twin Flames. All that was still unknown to them at that time.

Truth Must Come Out

For healing to take place this is essential. Everyone has a story. If you've suffered trauma in the past you must bring it out into to the light and don't ever push it down into the darkness. It can never heal there in the dark.

With true understanding comes growth. Angel looks back at how they travelled through this lifetime and all that they learnt. She is very grateful. She sees all the pain and loss now as gains. As she takes his hand she says: "Let all the pain drift away and may we both recognise it all as illusion that led us onto the path to love and forgiveness."

This realisation is essential to their healing. "Yes!" he responds. "We now walk into the sunset of life together." He looked deeply into her eyes. Probably more deeply than he ever had before when they were young and lived their lives so naively. Not knowing then that they had much to learn and pain to suffer.

When their eyes meet they fall into a pool of mystery. Why, oh why, were they destined to be so innocent? What if they had allowed the power of the fire and passion to release when they met?

That would have eliminated many problems that arose from that pure innocence. Why did they have to wait five years and their lack of knowledge cause angst?

It was their planned upbringing. Everyone around them was doing whatever they chose to do while they just loved each other but kept a step back all that time. They never thought to connect physically. Of course, with the knowing now, she realises that was all part of connection. It made them connect deeper because they had a problem to solve.

They worked on that problem for years and finally it simply broke free and everything seemed ok.

These Rings were first brought into existence for the purpose of not just one couple, but for their entire family and network of friends.

All will benefit. Everyone has a soul with a planned purpose on this Earth. Families are forever connected no matter what the situation looks like in the illusional world.

The Rings

If ever they needed confirmation that they are twin flames it is told in this story of 'The Golden Rings'. It was their way of cementing the flame connection way back just before they married. They bought two matching gold rings and had them inscribed inside. These words were to be prophetic. Their names and date of their marriage were also engraved with this inscription.

The words are:
"Hearts Truly Tied,
None Can Divide"

They lost sight of all this over the years and at some point Knight lost his ring while swimming in a lake. This was a major test. Somehow they continued on, being blind to everything and they never replaced his ring. But she now sees why that was. They both forgot those inscribed words that were prophetic for them.

Now that she is awake to their life and their pact she can see it clearly. It was to be significant for their reunion. The rings were to come into play once again with them joining the circle again.

The inscription was truly a spiritual guidance. The words are true. Their hearts are truly tied and no-one on this Earth can divide them. The only dividing or splitting was divine learning that we chose for ourselves.

63

The Effort in Matching

Matching the 'lost' male ring to the female Golden Ring after reunion takes great energy, awareness and passion for it to work. That's why it is part of their lifetime challenges. The more challenges, then the more is gained in knowledge and evolvement.

You see, if that female Golden Ring had not been kept all that time — for instance, if it had been lost, thrown away, sold or simply forgotten somewhere then the spell would have been weakened. The Twin Flame lovers would have lost a lot of their power. The spell put on them before birth, that they agreed to, gave them a tremendous amount of power in this lifetime together. Angel had clearly adhered to the pact subconsciously.

The power of the pact meant for Knight's ring to be lost at the bottom of that murky brown lake because then it still existed exactly where it had been at that time and place. It's fairly certain that in his sadness and anger when they split that he would have somehow gotten rid of it and its whereabouts would not now be known.

But now with all the planning that went into it, it can lie there and extend its power from that resting place. The extra time and energy it took the lovers to match and replace it strengthened their love, commitment and passion. Their awakening that caused them to remember its importance and power was in itself a miracle of the spell and pact.

Destiny wins again!

Their rejoining means they get a new replacement ring and inscribe it in the same way. The ring must match. *But Angel still has her original ring.* It was something she absolutely never let go of all these years. It was of major significance that she kept those two rings in a safe place. There is also the diamond ring. Not having his original ring that was lost simply means that they are adding to their reunion by consciously recognising the meaning of the rings.

They will add to the new awakening and joining by purchasing Knight's new matching ring with new inscription that cements what once was. This new ring being their new life. There is a parting of the ways for some and there is a new marriage in their Destiny for them. This pact cannot be broken in any way by anyone. Even the styling of the inscription must match. There is much detailed work to be done.

Spells Explained

They made a pact and the rings were under the spell. What does this spell accomplish? A spell will work wonders when made with the best of intentions. Spells that are truly endorsed by the heavens are divine interventions.

A spell takes over your ego human mind and directs it to where the chosen spell wills it to be. For example: Two lovers who could never part — the spell brings about thought patterns that cause a break, even seemingly against their own will. They can then become puzzled but they are helpless to resist the spell.

Other partners may appear to bring about enormous learning for one or generally both lovers. These people may be completely inappropriate but on the surface the spell makes it seem like new life and new love and obliterates all else.

Of course, it turns out that both lovers became involved with the utmost inappropriate other partners and went through much pain and suffering.

The special requirement for a true spell to work its magic is very simple. That is that it must remain in utmost secrecy and never be told. You quite simply cannot divulge any aspect of it to another person. That will contribute towards breaking the spell. It then may no longer be able to keep its power.

It must also be said here that there are no spells that can be implemented without the targets being in agreement to participation. That's why there is the meeting with the guides and the agreement by the One Soul to become Twin Flames and to their challenges in the coming lifetime together. This spell and pact is guided by the 6 Ascended Guides who are under the guidance of the 7th, who is JC and the highest being in existence. It shall be as it is said to be. All those years on Earth since 1946 and 1947, when these two were growing up, meeting and living their lives and challenges — they never gave a thought to whether they were living a destiny or not. It just never occurred to them. They just went with the flow — no matter whether it was joy or a deep challenge. The thing is, with the awakening of Angel, she has become far more aware of the next phase.

It is incredibly more difficult and a lot of work is to be done for it all to just fall into place. The job is now hers, and hers alone, to keep on going with the pact and its rules. This pact and its difficult jobs will bring the everlasting joy to both of them and their extended family.

He could easily make it better for her and take on half the responsibility by fully awakening. But it is now almost like the story of 'Sleeping Beauty'. He is asleep and slumbering with as much happiness as he thinks he deserves. He has no idea that he deserves far more. But the days on Earth are numbered for this Reunion to take place. It is coming, and it is coming right now. Angel's work in the manifesting process is about to be complete.

So although they both are now ageing and have managed diseases — she has now developed another more serious disease. Diseases match our lives. Her latest one is to do with the lungs. She is finding it harder to breathe towards the end of this long hard journey of finding her true Twin Flame all over again and making it known to him. Therefore she gained a lung condition. Also this is matching her destiny because the beginnings behind it date back to when she was 3 years old.

She has practised over a few years now how she can ask him a favour that she might expect him to refuse. But other times he has complied. She now has a huge major reunion favour to ask of him. When her writings of the prequel of their saga have finished and been bound as a book — that's when she will ask this huge favour. It is about travelling together to the 'forest of dreams' way out in the country area. They went there as teenagers before their marriage. She knows that going there again to repeat similar vows they made then will awaken him in a big way and that the golden particles will surround them.

She also has gifts to give him that relate to commemorating the places that are of importance. They are inscribed with engravings of co-ordinates that mean everything to both of them. This is one of the big surprises she has for him. It also will be that she has found the courage to speak her truth to him.

Angel feels the pressure of knowing she holds the key now. Once before long ago he held that key but she was not awake then. His anger and resentment drove him away then but those very emotions show that he loves her still to eternity. It's been genuinely verbally remembered that he has three times said the words that Angel is always and ever the love of his life. This knowledge spurs her on and on to absolutely never give up. To her dying breath she will not give up.

Her thoughts are "I can't live, if living is without you Knight".

She now commits all to fate. They will go with 'whichever way the wind blows'. But the guides know that even the wind is controlled and directed by the spell. So nothing can go wrong from this point onwards.

"We were once One as Two
But were torn apart by the gods

The pursuit and desire for another
to be One
Is called Love"

~~~

I am falling …

I am falling …

I am falling … in Love

*We are both destined to again
fall together
into the pool of love*

CHAPTER 9

The Jeweller: 1968

He concentrated on the heating and beating of the strips of gold. He formed the strips and then rolled them around the metal ring mandrel. Beating and beating till they were smooth and even. Then he joined the ends to make rings. He beat that join till it was smooth and matched the ring itself. He made one for a man and a smaller one for the woman. They matched each other and energies entered them from the heavens.

He polished and polished till they were a golden sheen fit for a grand love and a grand wedding. They were not too thin and would last far into the future. They were, in fact, very substantial and made into the thick shape as per instructions given to him from the guides. They had the strength and power to keep their inner energies burning. They had a slight curve from edge to edge. The finish is so glossy. They had a golden story beaten into them. They would be a story in their own right. Their connection to the Twin Flames is what made them alive. As they sit in the display cabinet in the shop they pulse out energies to attract the pacted Twin Flames to them on exactly the right date in time and space for this sacred event.

This jeweller was truly a Lord of the rings. He understood the importance of his job. He felt the sacredness of making these particular rings. He felt the fire and energy of the Twin Flames. This energy spurred him on with his job, working into the night.

He instinctively knew the One Soul of the Twin Flames. He knew of their innocence and purity. He felt it and he put that knowledge into the making of the rings. The rings are truly unique just as these two Twin Flame lovers are unique. Neither of them can ever truly join with any other partner in life but each other. This fact is decreed from the uttering of prayers and mantras from the universal field.

He knew these rings would languish in the shop till the right Twin Flames came along and purchased them. These two lovers were marked by angels to be the only ones for these rings. The shop co-ordinates:

-37.81504740784203, 144.9661685621699

He even knew they would be inspired and guided to have the chosen inscription put into the inside of each ring. These words were decreed in the beginning in Dimension 7.

The Twin Flames didn't remember this.

It was as if he knew their whole life story — and he did. Not only was the spell spun into the gold of the rings but the inscription held the spell also. It can never die.

They hold the perfectly matching frequencies that match the One Soul of the Twin Flames. Only when these frequencies match up after the split will the portal open for them. This is what allows them to match and reunite as was said in the beginning.

Even that one day one of those rings would fall to the bottom of the murky brown lake perhaps never to be found again. Eildon Lake, the playground and holiday place of campers and boaters. This event was planned on a higher level. We had no say in it. It was to mark the coming split for the Twin Flames. The event that would lead to spiritual evolvement, unconditional love and the destined reunion.

The fact that a new ring would be sought to match and repair hearts was preordained also. With the purchase of the new matching ring and the placement of it on Knight's finger — bells would ring and fireworks would explode. All this will occur on a different vibrational level and only the Twin Flame lovers can hear, feel and see this.

Energy will also pulse out of both rings that are now once again finally on the right fingers, in the right time and place, and also forever blending with their skin and their very body cells.

On this unique and awaited wedding day their actual physical heart wounds from their emotionally painful surgery will also blend and repair. Over time spent together they would continue to repair.

This jeweller's life and work was integral to this sacred couple. He loved his work and looked forward to each new spiritual assignment. As the rings are the focus of this story — therefore the Jeweller was extremely important also. He had to work with the spell and also be extremely talented and sensitive. He even wove their actual DNA into these rings. Knight's DNA will automatically be infused into the new ring when it is purchased. This will occur on a different vibrational level also.

The Lost Ring will be the focus of the fellowship that created it until this story is fulfilled. Its co-ordinates reverberate through time and space and past every star that was ever created and this is what they are:

-37.18521586219152, 146.06799308272713

~~~

CHAPTER 10

The Church: 1947+

*T**he Baptism** is the first time for her at the Church of Emmanuel. Her baptism was in 1947. This is the church her mother chose as her own. Its was not far from their family home — just a few streets away. It held magic for Angel, the twin flame female, all her life after that. She attended Sunday School and church services there for many years.

A black and white film of the life of Jesus she watched there stayed in her memory all her life. It was incredibly inspiring for her and she thought back to it many times over the years, whenever she needed that support and guidance.

Her mother attended this church regularly. Not every week but on special occasions she would go without fail. Angel recalls her mum's voice ringing out with all those older style hymns they both loved. Her mum daily sang at home as she went about her work. It made for a beautiful childhood.

This is the church where they married in 1968. Everything was beautiful on that day. The sun was shining. The memories are sweet. This church plays an important part in their lives. She remembers her sister being baptised there. Her dearest mum lay there in her white coffin for her funeral there. So births, deaths and marriages of the family were there.

This is the church. The One. It's still there and looks the same. Knight and Angel — yes they will marry there again and it will be their forever time. They will be planning a 'secret' wedding with only the required two people there as witnesses. Why? — Because it will all be a shock to family and friends that they are back together, let alone a new wedding. They will decide to be secret at the beginning. After-all it's all about them and always should have been.

There will be professional photos taken and perhaps a video for family to watch. Everything will be as it should be. They will also choose special meaningful music.

A short few weeks later they will organise a large dinner party where they announce their joining. There can be laughter and reunions for many who have become estranged in the family for no really good reason except stubbornness.

Church of Emmanuel

-37.906520 145.090060

"Knight this will be a special occasion for you for many more reasons. Over the years you have been misunderstood and maligned but this is the time for you to be back solidly into your own family," Angel tells him during the planning time together.

~~~

It is our challenge to wake up

To realise where our lost true love went

...

To recognise those unreal loves in our lives

CHAPTER 11

Angel & Knight: Pre 1946

*T*hey stood at the precipice of the universe. Glory was all around them as they looked down upon the Earth and its inhabitants. The sun and the moon were wonderfully visible to them. Holding hands they pledged their hearts to the plan and the destiny.

They are the One Soul but at this moment they appeared as the humans they would become. Looking directly into each other's eyes deeply and holding hands, they swore to their destinies. They also connected to The Golden Rings at this time. They saw those rings float before their eyes amid the blue beauty of the atmosphere and energies around them. Millions of stars shone throughout this blue.

They chose their parents at this time and pledged to meet up whenever the stars were aligned and sending them guided messages. There is now no possible way that they cannot meet as pre-organised at pre-birth.

Their meeting place was pre-arranged and the earth co-ordinates were destined. These numbers were to be etched upon their minds and souls. They are so important because if they are not adhered to and known, the meeting cannot take place. This is the place — this is the way. Exact co-ordinates below:

-37.909200, 145.083689

"Oh Knight, I will love you and all of you into eternity" spoke Angel into the stars.

"I love you with all my body, heart and soul," spoke Knight out into the universe, while at the same time, staring deeply into her soft velvety brown pools of eyes.

"You are unbelievably lovely," he whispered in her ear. "No, you are" she said. "No, you are" he echoed.

They pledged to return in every lifetime and be together in every possibility and every timeline. For eternity, to join in love as One. Each had the human attributes that the other desired most. Their physical magnetism to each other was unmatched. Their guides were emphatic in reminding them that they would be connected by love more than any others on Earth but they warned that they won't remember that they are to be split apart and cry many tears for each other. But always he is the moon and she the sea. The moon pulls the sea inwards.

They lived out their childhoods quite calmly and happily and then at the appointed time and co-ordinates on Earth – they met and they couldn't hear it, but there were gongs and bells ringing out in Dimension 7 on this day of all days. Later when they had spent 4 years together securing and cementing their relationship, they would enter that jeweller's shop in the city. A wedding was planned by them.

That city that was so much smaller than now, but it was theirs to own back then. They were there to seek out the golden wedding rings. They had no idea that the rings had already been chosen for them.

'And the gold for the rings spun around them' in the outer spiritual level where they first met and their One Soul split into Twin Flames before their births. It was joining them forever as they spun and spun, higher and higher up into their own vortex.

The jeweller showed them a few rings. Both of them felt the pull and the heat from The Golden Rings in the first tray they were shown. Knight's hands reached out to pick the ring that was his forever. After his choosing the jeweller showed Angel the matching ring. They were mesmerised and their eyes glazed over. Looking back they would not really remember this energy pull. But in the future they would become aware it was there. The Jeweller smiled to himself.

One evening, just after the purchase, they walked close together on a beach not far from home. There was no-one else there and the moon was amazingly bright and stars studded the midnight blue sky. Walking hand-in-hand they both suddenly felt an energy pull. Right in front of them a kind of hole appeared out of nowhere. There were spinning energies circling faster and faster. These energies contained all of the colours that existed. Each colour emphasised the other colours surrounding them.

It stopped them in their tracks. Knight exclaimed: "What is this Angel?" Angel was very still just gazing at it. They felt that pull and they walked closer to the hole. The centre was dark and swirling.

Then they both stepped into the wormhole. They spun around and around, still holding hands. The energies took hold of their minds. They went to a place that no human who ever saw it would remember it later.

They stood before what appeared to be a panel of higher souls. There were 6 of them sitting around a curved half-moon shaped table. A 7th higher soul was sitting in the centre of the group. All were wearing white and their appearance was soft and floaty. As they arrived to sit in front of the panel they did not have time to be afraid in any way. In fact, it was weird because time seemed to have stood still.

Knowledge was imparted to them concerning their entire lifetimes on Earth. They saw how they had been born, how they had spent their childhoods and early teens. They saw their pre-arranged meeting and how they were matched and also how they were actually One Soul. It was like watching a movie. Their minds, bodies and One Soul spun out.

Then they saw, watching with amazement, how their future lives would pan out on Earth. They saw the beauty, the love, the romance and they also saw the illness, pain, darkness and their separation. This brought tears to their eyes simultaneously. The leading white soul guide, the 7th, stopped them from allowing the tears to fall.

His voice was strong and deep but at the same time soft and light. "Never shed tears. This is your new life that you will spend together for the purpose of love and forgiveness." His voice seemed to boom out but was still filled with love. "We are giving you insight into how it all will be for the purpose of imparting into your bodies and minds, genetic information. This will fill your very cells. This will enable you to get through what seems like hard and dark times."

"There will be The Rings. You must take note of The Rings. They are the energy and soul of your life paths" said the leading guide. None of them had said if they had names. "There is a fellowship overseeing The Rings," he said. "The six guides, the leader, the two flames (who are one) and the jeweller. This makes for the number 9, which is the universal number."

His words seemed to echo now. I'm calling this guide a him but there is no gender here. These guides use their feminine or masculine energy depending on the situation and what it requires to get through to humans. These guides had been assigned specially to them and would follow them through their entire lifetime together.

There will be many times when they each will feel the pull of the guidance. The power of the rings is unleashed at the birth of Knight. He enters the Earth life first and awaits the birth of Angel — 4 months and 9 days later.

At her birth, the power of the rings increases two-fold. The reverberations ring out in the world. All those who are sensitive to vibrations will feel it.

Suddenly, just when they were beginning to get used to where they were, they spun again. They were suddenly pulled backwards. They were still holding hands. This made it seem like they were stabilising each other.

They spun back down what now appeared to be a tunnel. It was actually a vortex and its energies also spun. They became aware that there were other souls in the outer parts of the vortex. All looking at them with understanding and love.

They spun up again into the vortex together and it reflected their own true energies. They felt the love, the brightness. All at once they were One Soul, one being. Each felt the other's loves and fears and exact emotions.

It was overwhelming but at the same time it was as if it was expected all along. They were no longer two separate beings — male and female. It seemed only a short time since the start but it was exhilarating and amazing. At the same time it seemed to last forever. There was no time or space. There was just everything. Everything just was.

Next thing they were back standing on the moonlit beach. The waves were soft and gentle and the sound of them touching the shore was tinkling. The water was a soft glowing mix of blue and purple. They now had a new understanding of who they were and what their purpose was. Inside her mind Angel was timid, especially of the human world.

She had seen how the physical world was utter chaos and madness. She knew they both had to fit in somehow. Knight was strong, not timid exactly, but he never pushed his ideas onto others. To see them together as teenagers they looked just like they were from the angelic realms. There was even a white glow emanating from their bodies whenever they were together.

They were both born as naive and innocent humans. This was to contribute to their meeting and their relationship connection. It contributed also to the making of their human personalities. Neither would ever ask more of the other than they knew they could cope with.

Their wedding, after just over 5 years together, was a joining of virgin innocents. They had no idea what to expect from their joining. They just went in with trust and love.

That's all they thought they needed. They had forgotten that they had been shown absolutely everything about their lives here in detail. This wormhole travel was like their experience before birth in that it was a reminder just before they married. Both experiences were on Dimension 7. They still would not remember any of it when they were back in their physical bodies. Just like their experience before they were born. But this repeat experience was, of course, concentrated and remembered in their subconscious minds.

Back on Earth they followed the 'on the surface' conventions of the day. Although, unbeknown to them, no-one else was following this unspoken rule of life. This meant that they never gave in to their passions completely in those first 5 years.

In the pre 1946 time they had already pacted to be what they were. Their story is also about going from innocence to darkness and then back out again to be renewed and healed. It is a lesson to all who read their story and how they came through it all.

"Knight, you're the only person I've ever loved from the moment I first met you. From even that moment eons ago. This has never before happened to me. It's now obvious it's because we're Twin Flames. One Soul," Angel sighs.

~~~

I recall before that time

When we seemed to break

We had lost our connection

...

It broke my heart and
my mind

PART TWO:

The Play

Hearts Truly Tied

None Can Divide

(golden rings inscription 1968)

CHAPTER 12

In The Paranormal World
– Angel –

We *went on many adventures* into the paranormal world. It was always our destiny. We were guided to learn from these wonderful places. Hand-in-hand we literally flew all around endless dimensions. So many wonders passed us by. Sometimes we stopped to sit at the edge of diamond studded canyons looking out across valleys filled with flowers, streams, birds and butterflies.

The horizon was so far away, as we have never before seen these soft blue mountain peaks surrounding the valleys far away. A glowing light so bright as we've also never seen was in the far distance between two mountain peaks.

They took us to a purple dimension where we learnt all about our personal Vortex and how to enter it, be it and how to stay in it. The vortex refers to a swirling, spinning energy made up of all our thoughts, desires and creations. Once we are in it the universe must listen to all the vibrations we have put out. We float in a peaceful, love environment while there, so that everything in our destinies that we have manifested or desired will become the reality in our physical world too.

Another time we went to a forest filled with those colours never seen before. In the centre was a building made of pink quartz crystal. It had many spires, arched windows and one door. In the middle of an extensive garden was a clearing. In the clearing was a marble stand. On this stand perched two intertwining gold rings.

A message was imparted to our minds that these were The Golden Rings. The very rings that would be part of our compelling destiny on Earth.

Just then a beautiful white glowing horse rode by with a knight in the saddle. An angel sat behind him with her dark hair flowing out behind her. The whole scene was white and glowing. Just as suddenly the vision was gone. We both knew what it meant.

As we were standing before the marble stand with The Golden Rings on it — suddenly the angel was in front of us. I saw clearly that she was wearing a string of pearls. It was the short length style with graduated pearls. At once a memory flooded my mind — strangely a memory I had not yet lived through. I recognised those pearls. They were the pearls given to me by my Mum that I wore to our first wedding.

I thought to myself now, while suddenly being catapulted back to 2022: "Where are those pearls right now? Yes — the string is broken but they are all in an envelope in a drawer in my bedroom."

"I must go, as soon as possible, and take them to be mended." These pearls will naturally be used for our new second reuniting wedding. I now have almost everything ready for it. Except the dress. It will be made when I have chosen the material and been through my health transformation so as to be absolutely sure the dress will fit perfectly as did the first dress. Everything is then complete and packed away from prying eyes.

The Angel/Guide told us not to fear in our Earth life as we would always be connected and even if it seemed we had parted, that it was untrue. I never will fear to not be reunited with him.

We are once again in the far away dimension we started in. The guides are before us in their semi-circle standing beside each other. They are reiterating the value of the rings and the pearls. They represent the energies that connect us. Gold: it is the highest energy and Pearls: the beauty from the sea. Both the sea and any water connects Scorpio with Pisces.

Symbols and numbers rule the created universe. If we follow them we will always connect the way our destinies meant us to.

~~~

I've never known love
like ours

...

Knowing you're with me
Now and Forever
Makes everything ok

... Twin Flame

CHAPTER 13

Angel: Her secrets
– Angel –

*I*f you don't try, then you can't win! I will do my utmost in my endeavours to awaken Knight. I may embarrass or fail myself but I'm going ahead with all plans. Knight deserves it.

Who dares; Wins!

My main secrets are that I require a super demonstrative kind of love that is both true and romantic. Also I can easily fall apart when I imagine that the love that's so special and has found me seems to be falling apart.

Another one is that I can take just so much unhappiness and then my way out will usually end in me running away. I know this running away hurt Knight very much and I can see this easily now, but I could not back then. I'm fully prepared for the fact that Knight may need time to process his decisions. Although I'm aware that Knight is ripe for this very moment of transition in time. I know him well and I know I can predict his decisions and that he takes time to get there. I have the full faith of knowing.

We learnt that we should never have taken each other for granted back then. Our love should have demonstrably flowed every single day, every single moment — as I feel it now. As it is released now. We should have clung to each other every second. Not let problems and sickness interfere with us. That's how I feel about you but somehow the era and our upbringing (our fate) prevented the flow I now feel should be unstoppable.

I've always said in sorrow, Knight: "Why did I let you go?" But the clincher has occurred, as I've now changed my thinking to: "Why did we let each other go?" We are both responsible.

That is the true awakening. That's what really happened. We currently need to cling like magnets to each other from now on.

The spell and pact reacts to the very words I say to myself now. It reacts by making changes for us. Those changes can reverberate around the world making tiny changes for everyone, but will many notice? No, they will not really. Now what is created is the new world. That works where we remain together touching and blending forever into infinity. We must get to the Awakening Stage and stay there mindfully.

The spell has pinged! The pact exploded into millions of fireworks like stars. Many people in the world can see them. Many of them take inspiration from them. It is done!

I can say this to you Knight: Every single thing I did back then is not me. I would never make those decisions in our Now. I'm absolutely and positively aware that you know this now. I now look back to a black time I can't understand anymore.

Your new and recent partner (who seems to stand between us now) whom you may depend on in some way is not giving to you in a real way. You are still alone. I thank the guides and the spell for that, I breathe with genuine relief.

You just cannot be living or sharing with anyone right now — so that the reunion takes place. It is only I who will save you and no-one else can. It is the wrong timing for anything like this to even be. I must rid myself also of the partner who appears to be with me. It is all fake and must be turned to dust.

The only reason I seem now far more in love and passionate about us and only us has nothing to do with being without you for so long. It is to do with the spell that broke us for years and that spell brought about illusions. So now that I see through them, I see us as we really are. I still learnt a huge amount from mistakes and being deprived of you for so long. You are my other half so it's no wonder both our human bodies seem to be dying. It's the missing you days and nights that dry up and strangle my actual body.

Hear all this Knight and respond. You are also deprived and can turn that around anytime you have that Scorpio confidence powering out from you. Don't let age and illness stop you now.

Other secrets of myself were how I fell down into a deep valley over the years. Those years together, spending time together, going out, dating and just generally having the fun of teenagers in love had made me think that it would all go on forever without change. I did not factor in the life changes that break the pattern and strain people. Many don't last after these stresses. They break and never get back together. This was not even on the horizon for us — Angel and Knight.

But in our innocence, when finally embarking on our first pregnancy with both joy and trepidation — changes occurred almost immediately that we had never expected. Firstly: I was very ill during this first pregnancy. I suffered from a condition called HG (hyperemesis gravidarum) pregnancy. It was not then named to me but I suffered from constant nausea and vomiting and inability to eat well. It is quite traumatic and high risk.

On one occasion I collapsed completely and it was the first time I was given one of the drugs I reacted to all of my life after that. At a much later time in the pregnancy I became unable to cook food or eat much. Early in the pregnancy I had lost a lot of weight and one day when out shopping the engagement ring we had painstakingly chosen together fell off unnoticed. It was impossible to know where it had fallen and it was never found.

Lucky it was insured and Knight got another one for me. Later in our life after our first born was with us this 2nd engagement ring was also missing. This time we knew for certain it had been stolen from a drawer it was kept in. This was because late in pregnancy my fingers had swollen and it had to be cut off. It sat in that drawer waiting to be mended.

Also being insured, we once again consulted a jeweller and he presented us with another new one. I still have this one to this day. It is for the day when it will once again be used as an engagement ring for our reunion. Three diamond rings must also mean something. Such as each having a meaning: The 1st one our first love, 2nd our stressful years and the 3rd to be kept for our reunion.

My main secret in my life is I simply cannot abide any kind of life without romantic love within it. This is probably because I am part of a twin flame pathway. But my heart beats with sadness every day since I lost my true love. It's a devastating feeling, like falling into a deep crevice. Life seems so empty it's hard to try and look at daily miracles that exist around me. I know that for a time I thought I had found a new love but it turned sour and was fake.

The truth came out eventually and I am now creating the space in my life for you to come back, Knight. Love and closeness is coming to both of us.

It's coming! Do not be sad anyone. Love will always find a way, most especially if it is planned by a Twin Flame incarnation guided by spiritual beings, pacted vows and a spell of golden rings. We will not be alone for much longer. We must think positive every day and find beauty in the world every day.

I will ignore those who try to bring me down each day. To practice this difficult task is essential. We must now vow to 'live' each day and never be sad or lost again.

Another 'Grace' will save us

~~~

If it's not forever

Then it's not love

CHAPTER 14

First and Last: 1963-1968+
– Angel –

*A*ll *of our firsts came in this lifetime.* You were my first and you will be my last. That goes for both of us. All our firsts we shared together. That means nothing can separate us unless it is purely temporary and we come together again and again over many lives and particularly in this lifetime. No-one can ever take that away from us.

These are our firsts and our memories. They are our start in life. They link us forever. Think on all the firsts you could possibly have when you met someone special at age 16. Whatever you can think of, we can claim as ours.

We learnt and grew from each other. Think on it all: first and only true love, first house, first furnishings, almost anything you think of is at some point a first. First in organising our two lives to blend. First romantic love and first physical love.

First to realise staying apart was not planned for our fate. Whenever a first resulted in part failure we have never ever divulged any of this to another soul. It is our life and our memories. We protect each other from the intrusion of others — as it should be.

All this was also vowed before our birth here. We were happy to learn everything from each other in this chosen twin flame lifetime.

We've been extremely fortunate even though many of our firsts were passion, pleasure, building a home, births, deaths, losses, joys and connection — we also shared illness, pain and a split in our relationship.

We shared the horrors of new relationships that were never going to work for either of us. We both shared the mistakes, pain and sorrow when we realised that being apart and being with others who could never really know us or show real love was what we had unwittingly chosen.

I can list more of them here. It will be all of our firsts. I am grateful for every one Knight.

First love, first physical connections and wonders, first joys going out and loving life, learning to drive, first jobs, first planning for engagement, first buying of the rings, first planning for a wedding, first planning for our lives together and building a new house.

First painting and finishing our house and the decoration and buying of furniture. Also our first record player and first buying of a vinyl album. I remember it well. You chose it Knight. It was 'Johnny Cash'. A 75 album with all his hits. Setting our own house up was our joy and we put everything into it.

Wow! I can then list other firsts that were more anxiety producing and scary. We had years together, working and building up our house. All our friends and relatives were having their first children. We still did not have anything like that on the horizon.

But according to the spell we had very much in the way of challenges on our horizons. Life's challenges can be extremely painful and different for many people and their various paths. We chose our pathway for the good of all. So we became inundated with challenges we were not prepared for. They tore us apart.

~~~

Twin Flames never meet by accident

...

How could that be when they are

already within each other

...

CHAPTER 15

Knight: Terrifying Ordeals

*E*ach of the twin flames went through terrifying ordeals. These are their pre-chosen challenges in this lifetime. For Knight, the first ordeal was when he came home one day to find Angel had left. She didn't leave any kind of sign that this was what she would do.

She left to escape the fact that she thought she had lost the love of her life. Both Knight and her had become estranged over a number of years. It all left her feeling bereft. It's now known that she was lost and under the spell at that time. It pulled her into a whirlpool from which she could not escape. This was planned so neither could escape all the events coming towards them.

It seemed that life was spiralling out of control for both of them. Later, down the long track of years, she would see that it was all a huge mistake. But this mistake was only on the human earth life level. It was still part of their own pact.

The early years together were so innocent, pleasureful and full of plans.

They both had to be brave to even contemplate this lifetime together and accept all the pain of the ordeals. It is always easy to be brave before the incarnation.

The immediate aftermath of this sudden splitting from Knight's point of view, was not in any way known to Angel. She was in a dream state that stopped her realising. For Knight this was a horror state. He was lost to the world for a time. But because he is a Scorpio he started very soon to pick himself up to a degree.

But that is when his first nightmare of an ogre appearing in his life started. In the state he was in he was easily fooled by a female that cropped up in his life. She proceeded to take over his life and family home. She was completely unsuited to him and unmatched. She was the second major challenge. She also proceeded to pick fault with Angel and their children and tried to take over the Twin Flames working out their family and legal aspects of it all. It took him nearly 2 years to wake up to all this and split with her.

The first time Angel saw any kind of sight of this ogre she was horrified for Knight. Angel started to feel deep sorrow at what was happening to Knight. Years later she wished she had gone back to him then.

But the spell didn't allow for that yet. Even the Golden Rings still had not rejoined their energies from their own split. From their own separate places where they lay apart. Angel's Golden Ring was in her possession still and Knight's ring was at the bottom of the lake in its resting place. This ring in the lake knew its path in this story of two lives. It was to remain dormant for many years.

The Golden Ring that Angel had with her became sometimes actually forgotten. But it was always there (in the back of her mind) and she would catch sight of it every so often. She knew the importance of keeping it safe. That's really all she knew about it then. She didn't know why still.

Knight's ring lay forgotten even to the Twin Flames at the time it disappeared. They did not attempt to replace it at that time. They currently now wonder why, but it was also in the plan and the spell. Their human forms cannot necessarily understand the why of all this.

But with Knight's loneliness and his star sign that requires love in his life he almost immediately met another dark ogre. This time she was known to others and he was warned. She fooled him well and truly just like the previous one did. This time he married again. He should have been awake. This one did not care for his children that lived with him and they did not like her either. She was mean spirited. The two years they spent away from their mother were sad and lonely with Knight putting all his attention on the two new loves that would both let him down meanly.

Many times he would lament that no-one one is like my Angel. But instead, he remarried, and then his children all went to live with their mother, Angel. He then stepped back out of all their lives. For a long number of years neither Angel nor his children even knew where he was living. He stopped all contact. A typical Scorpio will retreat when they are hurt or they have lost something important to them.

But a long way down their life pathways he let it be known that he had left this marriage as she was very hard to love and tried to prevent him seeing his children. He continued an association of sorts with her but moved out.

No-one in his family really knew that the marriage had failed as he never spoke of any details. Most mistakenly assumed that the marriage had gone on for at least ten years. Angel thought this and this thought prevented her from letting Knight know how she really was still connected to him. Under the coverup of the spell they were under, her true feelings still did not come forth. But this is a time that they could have reunited.

This reuniting was not to be as it still wasn't the right time. There were quite a few more challenges to go through yet. Things that would try their strengths and abilities far more even yet. There were also many things to discover about each other and their true connection.

Everyone has a pathway in life
They are all different and individual. There will be many challenges but you won't know when they will turn up or turn bad. It can be very disconcerting and take you unawares.

Except for Twin Flames who will always join their pathway back together again.

~~~

The truth of our everlasting connection

...

I was blinded for a while
Now I'm awake and can see

...

It's You & Me

CHAPTER 16

Angel: Her Own Dark Ordeals

*A*ngel *had her own ordeals* to go through. To the world it appeared that she just went off with someone new, got remarried and life was working out for her. Nothing could be further from the truth. She was truly fooled right from the start but she could not see it. There were signs and warnings along the way right from the beginning. Despite what had occurred and how she had left — she was still innocent and naive to the ways of the world and her own part in this world.

Angel Was Ripe For Victimisation
She thought she had lost her true love. After all there were many years since the lovers had acted out their love for each other. They had changed, both of them. They were estranged and had been for quite a while.

She was hugely mistaken in imagining that this new ogre (sent from their Destiny Plan) was a love interest — even some kind of saviour. It was all elusive illusion. She was well and truly fooled into falling in with the life plan. She had no idea. Then she was imprisoned for 30 years. This is so hard to believe. Surely a victim would wake up well before this. It's not that she never woke in all this time. It was a slow process and being who she is — an angel and also a Pisces — it was hard for her to wake to the fact that she had to get away. She was afraid of making even more mistakes. How many more people could she feel guilty of hurting?

So she stayed — almost in a trance. Today, in the Now, she wonders how could she have ever let life change the taste of love for her. It seems inconceivable to her now as it would have in the 1960s.

She thinks back now and realises how many times she could have run to Knight and he would have been there waiting for her. Opportunities, but lost because of her mistaken ideas of how things really were for both of them. Neither of them could see the truth and the light and then there were many times that the door could have been opened.

She realised at some point far earlier than Knight could ever have imagined, that everything was wrong in their world. This is the time when she fell deeply into her 'dark ordeal'. They both suffered separate ordeals but these dark times will always meet in the middle and continue dark until they realise to combine their pain and tears to escape. She began to feel imprisoned. She knew it was her decision that got her there. Pisces hate to be trapped.

The Spell Intervened

It intervened when Angel failed to wake up years ago. She was semi awake but unsure of making changes or even if she could. Did she have the courage? She imagined her fate was sealed. No, it actually never was.

The spell caused the partner to pull away from her and make her feel alone and unloved. Unknown to either of them, he had a problem that caused this. These are the awakening years when she realised fully and awake that Knight was her true love. She could not understand why she had let go of him. She now wants to grab him and never let go — ever.

She had now gone way past some of the moments in time when they could have reunited. The spell is programmed to intervene during such events. The time was still not right. The full lessons had still not been learnt.

If they reunited during this time, then it is fully possible they would have broken apart again and not awakened at all.

~~~

It's about the Fire

of Life

...

And the communing

from The Rings

...

CHAPTER 17

Dark Night of the Soul: Knight

ay by day the turning began. He is gradually awakening. It is known that he, Knight, was always seeking her out in the early years. Then he eventually went into hiding and none of them knew where he was or what he was feeling. Angel's intuition of Knight is extensive and she realised later how hurt he was. Hurting makes people run away.

Knight Hits Rock Bottom. He has been approaching this dark place for years now since long before 2016. He thinks he is happy, that he has an apparent good life and he is content. This is another illusion. He has started the downward travel to depression. On the outside he is always happy but this hides his true feelings. He connects to people easily and is always seen as a happy personality with a lot to say.

He is headed towards the place called 'deathly shadows'. This place is so very dark because the moon has abandoned it. Not many shadows can be visible but those that are, are deathly and must be avoided. No-one knows what creates those shadows.

The forest is so dark not even a sliver of a glow from the moon can penetrate. He stands alone at the entrance to this darkness. He is not afraid but he still does not comprehend why he is there. He is not awakened to this but once he delves deep into the forest and appears to become lost, he will understand.

He enters with trepidation because he is aware that this is his final challenge. He is strong and supported by the guides and the vortex from long ago. He tentatively feels this strength but he has still not unleashed its full power. There is no need to as of yet. He is completely unsure of what he may encounter in the centre. He steps through — sometimes walking into tree trunks that are black and unseen. The dark trees sway towards him, they seem to be alive and to be working against him. He somehow remembers to push on and ignore fears.

And now, unlikely as it seems to him, he hears the dark trees whispering. What else can it be? He sees no people in the forest. Only darkness, enveloping trees, dark trunks close together, leaves rustling in the dark shadows, no light and barely any movement at all.

He is now truly aware that he has entered the dark place of shadows he was warned about. The surrounding entry circle called deathly shadows is

116

only the beginning — it is not the centre. The Shadow of Death place where he will be challenged and hopefully he will gain power over fear is the unseen and unknown centre.

"I will not heed this darkness and place of fear" he whispers hoarsely to himself. Fear taking his normal voice away from him. But he does not notice this. He notices nothing but the fear taking over him.

And then, to his fear and astonishment, he hears what seems to be an army of horsemen riding fast through the forest. These will be the fake people he will meet in his journey after his Split from Angel. They will run roughshod over the top of him, if he allows it, relentlessly until such time as the suffering has to end and he has woken up.

"Why, oh why had she left?" he cried this to himself. Forgetting that perhaps he had left her without support emotionally for many years. He had not meant this to be. It just happened. He had no idea that it was all pacted and empowered by the spell. He was still not awakened to remember all this that had occurred before his birth.

He still could not even imagine that there had even been a time before his birth where they had been together in the far dimensions and that they had held hands and joined in the spell for the future and for their destiny to be fulfilled.

Those horsemen quickly approached where he stood in the forest. It was almost impossible that they could fit into this forest as the trees grew close together. Suddenly he saw them riding very fast right at him. They looked like ancient warriors. Carrying their metal shields as they road those horses violently towards him.

The roar of that group riding was intensifying in his ears. He immediately attempted to hide behind a group of five trees that were closer together than some of the others. They rushed past him but soon after they realised and turned back. He ran and ran now. He felt this was the run of his life. The rough and fearful breathing from his desperate running caused him great pain in his lungs. Fear gripped him like a vice. But as he ran he then recalled how he had learnt to defy fear and be calm. He sweated.

This didn't stop him from still running as fast as possible. They were almost upon him. He suddenly wondered what would happen if he just stopped running away? Perhaps they didn't even exist. His fear may have created them.

Suddenly in the midst of his fear and running he stopped dead in the forest. There was silence. Even the hoof beats and clanging of the armour was not heard. The blood thirsty grunts and cries of the evil horsemen were no longer there and could no longer threaten him. He turned. All he saw was the multitude of massive trees. They now murmured softly in his ears. Their soft sound was music to him. They softly pushed and pulled him towards Angel and towards love.

They Found the Secret Together

If they both run away through those deep dark woods together and combine both their love and strength then that's how they will win and escape. It must always be a joining of their One power to win through any challenge or fear. As currently they are not reunited, they both start their journeys separately but they are pacted to meet in the darkness before escaping together.

Now as they run together, holding hands, their power connects. All of a sudden, in the middle of their forest run, mirrors appeared all around them. Tall narrow mirrors side by side so that they touched each other. They stopped running in their tracks to avoid hitting them. They stared and turned around and around looking at their own reflections in wonder. Without warning, a part of the sun shone through some overhead tree gaps. It brilliantly reflected a powerful light onto them and caused flares from each mirror. At first they are temporarily blinded from the powerful beams.

They eventually realised they could come to no harm while being surrounded by these mirrors and with the light shining into them. It bounced off the mirrors and entered their entire beings — their very souls were lit. The light entered every cell in them.

The sound of the pounding hoof beats that chased them down had dissipated into silence. Suddenly they realised their joined energy and love had shown them both the light and the way. They are then instantly lifted high up out of the dark menacing forest. There are no creatures chasing them anymore. They never really existed. Only their fears existed. This is the life metaphor and they have now seen it and they know it and they have survived.

The Metaphor of Sleeping Beauty
In actual fact, in this instance sleeping beauty is the male, Knight. Angel is already awakened. It is she who must kiss Knight so that his true love awakens him. He wakes from his long nightmare to see the face of his twin flame whom he instantly recognises.

He realises she saved him and that she saved their love. She inspired Grace in their lives. It is their love that is their symbol and gift to the world. Wake up Knight — your tears and Angel's need to be dried. Surely on your reunion they need never fall from your eyes again.

The Two Young Virgins. These two who are virgins ran hand-in-hand through that dark forest. They didn't realise there had been a shift in both of them — in their One Soul. This meant their running and their fear had come to an end. They became calm and looked around. Right in front of them they saw leafless trees, multitudes of them, all white, just like silver birches. Their trunks and their branches were beautiful like carved white wood. "You must have been searching for me ... you sent me signals ... messages on the wind, from the sun and in the sky floating on the clouds" she said to him now.

Her dress pure white and her heart beating strong ... Just like 1968. White silk and delicate tulle made by a mystical dressmaker to fit her exactly. It had become miraculously clean again and the torn pieces were back together. It was perfect once again. Now the light was also upon him. The moon had appeared fully round and bright and shone its beams through those now friendly looking trees. Angel has discovered a portal that leads back to 1967. At some point she takes Knight through that portal before he awakens and before the inevitable reunion.

There are a number of portals and she shows them to him. They all come from accessing places they've been to in the 1960s. This takes them back to their original true love that can never be broken. They enjoy everything that was in their lives from that time while visiting the past.

They pocket some of their greatest memory particles from their visit and take them back with them to 2023. Those particles change everything including time and space. They have that secret within them now as Angel has enlightened Knight as to the time travel and the seeds left behind that can be brought into the future.

~~~

Even before that, when we still had at least some physical connection

...

I could not remember for a long time why I left

...

My big regret covered it up

CHAPTER 18

Dark Night of the Soul: Angel

Her own dark night is really many events. Overall the entire time away from her Knight, whom she loves deeply, has been a 'roller coaster ride'. She can see herself clinging to the rail of the roller coaster, her legs flailing out behind her, as it flies along the rail. It is constantly dipping up and down as it goes. She's outside the roller coaster trying not to let go. That is her life now. Being pulled along, clinging to the edge, as her silken hair flies out behind her, and she lives this fear daily.

Knight, more than likely, imagined for many years that Angel was happy to be away from him and living a good life. This was never her true reality and each day, week, or year it all got worse. She wanted you and only you.

"Oh Knight: If you could ever get me off this roller coaster please do it now. I'm sick, I'm dizzy and 'get me outta here,'" she pleads.

Dark night of the soul is just that: so very dark and filled with fear and tears.

She's been up, she's been down, she's been all over the place. Her emotions and feelings have been scrapped.

If only Knight knew she wanted to go back to him so far, far long ago. The strength and commitment to saying so, that she now has, was lost on her years ago as she still retained that naivety and lack of confidence from her younger years. She was afraid. She is no longer afraid and when she next meets up with Knight she will be saying what needs to be said for the benefit of them both.

Angel's time in the capsule of challenges was coming to an end. She literally could not hold up much longer. She was weakening. Knight was strengthening (even though he could not feel it) as it was to be in the pact and plan. He could be strong enough now to pluck her out. He just had to have that commitment and realise who they were to each other.

If they visit together one or more of these places his mind and soul will awaken. They will temporarily be transported into another dimension while standing together on the Earth where sacred pacts were made. She can hasten and strengthen this energy release if she also wears the jewellery that is sacred to them both. He must also *touch* the ring she is wearing. On the instance of his *touch* the spell of The Golden Rings will spin out. This spinout will surround them both and pull them into its vortex tightly where they will then feel that energy engulf them. Those golden rings hold such power as to bring them into their original true connected love.

Angel chose it

It is now clear. "I chose to fall into the swirling whirlpool," she acknowledged. "I went into the quagmire. Yes, it's true that I was blind." But when she started to recognise her wrong choices — why didn't she find her way out? Because — well, because — she felt stuck and unable to move. You could say paralysed.

Angel had fallen into amnesia for many years. She 'forgot' her true love. It was caused clearly by the spell and pact and the pushing and pulling of her energies to the point where she could not make her own choices.

In her new awakened state she can simply not relate to this time of forgetfulness. She is now fully awake and has access to all the energies that crowd her mind from sacred places and vows they had participated in. She is getting impatient for them to be together as is already destined.

We know she remarried after leaving Knight all those years ago. At the present time she realises she cannot relate to this second person at all any longer. He is causing an imbalance in her energies daily now.

They live an unconnected life but together. She feels the chains as if she is imprisoned. All this because her true love has gone. Gone for now but not forgotten and not left behind. It was all illusion that their one and only connected love had gone.

"Knight please come — please rescue me — please also rescue yourself from the binds we are in." Angel connected with Knight and the universal field. "Our life ahead is filled with joy and passions."

Daily she utters affirmations to work with the universe, the Law of Attraction and manifesting. She knows these laws well from her past. But this was now a massive assignment. She knows persistence and seeing the outcome as if it has already occurred is the secret.

Time is no longer real to her. Her mind constantly tells her to hasten the reunion. Time is one long space-time continuum now.

Knight has become involved with a new partner in life. This relationship is not pacted or sacred. He clings to it out of fear and loneliness. Because Knight is a Scorpio he is not suited to live alone without love. This person can in no way fulfil him. There has been no real commitment within this relationship. It is this total commitment that he desires and possibly unknown to him it must be with his one true love only. His long years without Angel played on him badly. He came to the conclusion that she was not going back to him because all this time has gone by. He had forgotten their pact made before they were even born.

"Why did I not awaken long ago?" cries Angel to herself. She now has a huge job to awaken him but she is supported at all times by the guides in spirit. She knows deep down that her not awakening earlier was also a sacred pact. His new relationship, which is clearly not really new anymore, will crumble and fade. For a very good reason — she has not joined him completely.

Any time we access past spaces and actions we are not being stuck in the past if we control the energies properly but instead we are using the energies from back then. This is a choice. You must deliberately not fall into any negativity from the past but only access the good and bring it into the Now so you can use it still. Those energies travel to the Now in our minds as we access them through our mind right now. Accessing the good energies from the past must be deliberate for it to work in the now.

"I want to feel the luxury of you brushing my hair. I loved it then and I desire it more now. You even washed my hair in the bathroom basin in Colbinabbin," she recalls. Such simple pleasures that cause the passion to soar higher and higher.

This mountain she must climb. It looks higher and higher now. The rocks are in her way — the challenges far and beyond more difficult. Her physical strength is not what it used to be but she must ignore that. She's climbed mountains before in her life but they didn't have Knight at the finish line. That's why this mountain she will climb and never give up on. Never will she give up.

Angel sees the walk in the Colbinabbin bush now as it was then. She is there with him walking, holding hands. They turn to each other, both hands outstretched towards the other and clasping. This time can never be forgotten because it stays with her and has returned in her mind many times.

Their vows are whispered on the wind. This can never be erased now as the wind has caught the vows and will keep those whispers eternally

Could this moment last for infinity? The new Colbinabbin walk in the forest. The inevitable kiss — it can go on and on and never end.

They will now return to this walk in the bush. It will be Now, in 2023. They will access the power of those vows and catch the wind once again. That whisper on the wind will catapult them again into their vortex, spinning and spinning and catching them into their existence, the spell and the pact.

Her *Dark Night* approaches now. It will take her deep until she can bear no more. That is the only way to rise — to reach rock bottom. She also finds herself in a dark forest. It is not like the one Knight was in. At first it looks colourful and friendly. There are creatures that seem to befriend her all around. She feels at ease now.

But … very soon as she walks into it, it becomes very, very dark. The trees are now menacing. Fear rises up from within her heart. She hurries now, but falters and falls many times. Her knees are now bleeding profusely. She barely notices this.

Angel's dark night of the soul was her imprisonment. She is in a wooden square box. Big enough to stand in and around 4 metres by 4 metres. The strong sticks crisscrossed all around it. There was just a pile of hay. Presumably to sleep on perhaps. She awoke from her unconsciousness in this jail. Her white tulle Angel dress was dirty and in tatters. Some of the ogres came and entered this cage and threw her to the ground. They injected her against her will. She fell into a deep coma.

Eventually coming out of the coma she realises she must take action to get to her love. "Knight," she screams loudly. Knight is in another part of this very same menacing forest but very far to the other side of it. Her voice echoes across to his ears. Helped by the winds blowing.

He is still running from the creatures that seek to rip him apart. She then managed to make a hole in the netting and escape.

Looking quickly behind her she becomes aware that dark fearful creatures are also following her at a fast pace. She has never felt such fear before in her life. She wonders whether to give in and fall to the ground and let them devour her. "Please Angel," the angelic voice whispers in her ear. "Do not fear and do not give up."

She can see the angel guide now. This angel now holds out her hand for Angel to hold onto. She pulls her along faster and smoother. They are back and joining Knight in his own dark forest challenge.

The angel almost drags her but it does not hurt at all. She feels she must continue on with this angel that has appeared out of nowhere to help her. She knows she can never reach her goal and her love if she even hesitates to a small degree.

"I am taking you to Knight. Both your journeys are now nearing the end. The end is but the beginning also," she tells her.

She looks back again and those creatures have become even more evil looking. "Just remember, Angel, these creatures are but illusions that contribute to your transformation. When you can no longer see them at all, that's when you realise they don't really exist."

On and on they travelled through this dark forest. The trees became fewer and further apart until there was a kind of clearing. From across the clearing she could see someone running fast towards them. It is Knight. He is being also chased by the same dark evil creatures. Angel runs towards him, leaving her helping angel behind. Only Knight can mean everything to her now.

Suddenly from the left of her she sees Knight's beautiful silver white horse run into the central clearing. Also quite suddenly she sees Knight has possession of a magnificent shining silver suit of armour. He puts this all on very quickly and mounts his horse. He is now fully ready to exercise his true powers. He is Scorpio the Phoenix now.

As he pulls Angel up onto the horse behind him, they are now a wonder to see, riding through the dark forest away from the clearing but still with the evil ones chasing them. Her version of letting fear go is this horse with its pure white mane, Knight in his shining armour and Angel in her flowing white tulle dress as they all ride away from danger.

Knight is actually now playing out the danger for Angel to get through as he previously stopped dead in the forest, cleared his fears and the evil ones disappeared for him. Angel now has to get there too.

They have both reached rock bottom during these long years which were filled with darkness and depressive failure. This is the catalyst for change. They were sent downwards deliberately so that they can realise where they have fallen and to test that they have the strong will to rise again together. When you are at the very bottom you can go no lower unless you relinquish your soul completely. They both have within them the power to never ever allow this to occur. It is a soul gift to them before birth and it is their inner knowledge.

Angel now has the eye of the tiger
Now when it comes to Knight. She will never take that tiger's eye off her target. He is hers now and forever and she is his. Anyone could look deep into her tiger brown eyes to see how they focus on what is important to her at the time. Like a tiger does while stalking as a predator for its next meal as in nature.

Dear God
They are now mesmerised and standing in the centre of the suddenly appearing mirrors that they experienced in Knight's ordeal. The Twin Flames have been suddenly lifted into the white cloud-like place. The feel is so soft and serene.

They are both lying together and being cradled by a pair of huge arms and hands. This experience comes to them together at the end of their ordeals.

Also the arms are symbolically white. There was a whispered voice telling them they were being healed. That their hearts, minds and souls were being healed at that moment and gave instructions to please lay back together holding hands and relax into pure peace. Their hearts are also sealed together now.

They both went through different versions of the deep dark forest of fears and also their meeting up. So now, they are both rising out of the danger and once both their energies and minds are on the same level and on the same path then they will rise all the way back to Dimension 7.

This is when they will recall absolutely everything about planning their lifetime here with the spell and the pact with the spiritual guides.

They will also recall where they are heading on their path into infinity together. All it takes is for both of them to realise their power.

The Healing Time

They are both now experiencing the time together now of lying, side by side, and being cradled by the pair of huge white arms and hands. There was that whispered voice telling them they were being healed — that their hearts, minds and souls were being put back together and healed at that very moment. They were hearing and experiencing it all simultaneously this time.

This was truly the culmination of their dark times being won over and their reward had arrived.

~~~

That time way back beyond us
That time when we seemed to
break

...

I recall before that time
We had lost our connection

...

It broke my heart and
broke my mind

CHAPTER 19

The Hidden Doorway

*T*here's *a hidden doorway* in this story. The two people involved must first find this door. Then after that they must find out how to open it and walk through. Only at that precise moment will they know what is on the other side of it. Until that very time and that discovery they make together they will remain imprisoned.

Angel has already seen it and it wasn't in a dream — it was a proven vision. She knows what the door looks like because of previously seeing it. It is heavy wood that is carved. It seems blue but with dark edges. It's image gives the impression that it is very old. She can no longer recall whether the door had a straight top section or if it may have been cathedral shape carved. This vision was many years ago.

She now knows there is a secret to opening it. Not just anyone can open it and go through it. It is very heavy and there is a thick metal handle there inviting anyone to open it.

The handle appears to have a rope pattern to it.

If you're not ready to go through this door and you reach out and touch it you will get an electrical shock. The first time Angel saw it she reached out to open it. She touched it. This electrical shock was instant and it threw her backwards by around 2 feet. She felt herself go through the air.

She has never forgotten this door. It appeared to her the evening on a day she had spent many hours earlier learning deep meditation from a guru. It was the very first time for her to go very deeply into a meditation without anything disturbing her deep state of mind.

This door vision appeared to her when she was not alone and the person with her testified to her that she jumped suddenly backwards by a few feet like she had touched electric power somehow. This witness person knew nothing of the door vision and is what is known as a 'non believer'.

This experience has remained in her memory forever and she knows it is the pathway. She has never seen it again but she knows that she will. Its importance has followed her from that first time she saw and touched it.

It will come again and she will be with her Twin Flame and they will be ready next time. The door will open then. As soon as they have advanced high enough spiritually the door will appear. The vision beyond it will be astounding and beyond what they have ever seen before.

This vision will surpass even the amazing Dimension 7. It may not even appear to them until a long time after their reunion. It will be at the time they are about to go into infinity together.

That's when they will walk through into their destiny together. There will be no troubles, no fears and only love can exist there. Their own love is eternal and will last into infinity.

~~~

After all the loss and

all the pain

...

We deserve all the

happiness and all

the love again

...

CHAPTER 20

Becoming Calm: 2019-2023
– Angel –

My Twin Flame is coming to me — as is supposed to occur. Now that I know this I can be calm and accepting. I don't need to worry about where my other half is. It is you. My flame is not lost and never will be. Even though you appear to be with another right now I still keep my faith in the pact.

I also learnt that when you meet your Twin Flame they absolutely 'never' disappear from your life. They are with you for forever and far into eternity. They cannot ever be lost.

There are times, Knight, when the fact that you're not with me makes me physically sick. You would have surely seen this when we first split. I became very ill and ended up in hospital. Why couldn't I have woken up then? Why?

For a while after my Running Phase and Our Split I spent quite a bit of time 'forgetting' all about our connection. Looking back I can realise why this occurred. I needed to be in the forgetful stage for all the learning to exist for me. If I had not gone into the forgetful phase I also would not have left.

But, if so, we would not have followed our planned Stages in this Flame incarnation.

I'm sure you also went into this forgetful stage years ago too, or were you all along running from hurt and pain and hiding. I think you partly woke up for quite a few years but I, for reasons I couldn't control, did not see this.

Hello soul mate! Hello Twin Flame! Our flames arise from the heart of the One Soul and spread to eternity while blending together with the highest 'passion' that exists. We now have the opportunity to rejoin and complete our life journey. All it takes is for both of us to become awakened.

We must both also remain calm. We both need to put the effort into practising calmness in our daily lives but at the same time we must be faithful to our inevitable reunion. We must also be knowing.

~~~

*It looks like I'm swapping
back to you*

...

That is not the case

...

*It is that I'm now seeing
the Truth*

The Golden Rings

CHAPTER 21

Recognising Us: 1963+
– Angel –

*I*t's *important to know* and recognise that we are Twin Flames. I look back and I see at our first meeting while still very young that we were innocents. We were incredibly naive. But we were lovers all the same. That holding in of the true fire and passion of our union was completely from being innocents.

Recognising our innocence is recognising our 'divine' angel connection. Although naive, we still had deep healing to go through. This is what we look for when searching for the truth of a Twin Flame relationship. This will not be the case for every Twin Flame situation. They vary greatly.

But I now see our innocence and angel-like sacred relationship as the very foundation of what was to come later. Although we went through the pain and separation we learnt to be innocent once again. You can't remain unknowing and still learn all that you incarnate to learn. You need to be knowing.

Sacred Identity

In everyday karmic relationships the partners relate to each other 'humanly'. These other relationships work through the ego. But our relationship was sacred from the very start. It was magic all along. We can both look back to see this now. In the beginning there was never any ego power stands. Later when going through the lead-up to separation there was the appearance of those deep dark emotions to heal. We mirrored each other by going through various emotional breakdowns. But we also went through our own separately. We had no idea how to join forces to combat our own breakdowns together.

During our break I was eventually led down the spiritual learning path. The catalyst for this was the passing of my mother. It was instant that I turned to learning all about spiritual matters. I had previously not had any overt interest. I have no recollection of relating any of that to my actual life before. Suddenly I was catapulted into this new understanding of life, death, love and the spirit.

I have since had a number of spiritual 'events' in my life. Including 'out of body' experiences and dreams. I have been challenged by some of the things I went through and saw.

It's important that I realised when our soul split and our relationship fell apart that I for one was seeking fulfilment on the earthly level. But I only realised this many years later.

I was shown fairly early on in the new relationship I ran to that it was not ideal at all but I ignored that. I had my head in the sand. I behaved in a way that was alien to me and who I really am. I thought I was alone and I was accidentally entangled with a soul whom 'appeared' also to be seeking the same thing. A lost soul who I felt drawn to for the purpose of both healing that person and myself, just turned up in my life.

I was not ever actively seeking any person.

But what I was doing was running away from home because I had not awakened to our true Twin Flame relationship. I had lost sight of the truth. I had suffered chronic illness on various levels and I had lost my way as well as my identity. I could not 'see' who I was or who 'we' were.

I see now the Twin Flame identity of our life relationship. I see back and there is a view like looking at a slide show of when we met. I know the place and the feel of it. It was instant. I could smell it. I am it. There was no just slowly going into a relationship when we first met. It was on fire from the start. The only thing was that we were both young and unable to show outwardly just how much fire was inside. I feel it now when I look back. I feel the time we wasted by not allowing that flame to burn fiercely like a wild beast. This was through naivety and lack of knowledge. The fire was there but we held back, letting love just smoulder quietly.

Beautiful Memories: As already stated in the Chapter (Meeting) the very first meeting reverberates in my mind over and over. Starting early with the memories that stay in my mind forever and ever. The day we met. I now go through these memories once again. My friend and I were attending typing lessons to upgrade our skills at a local Technical School. We would catch the bus straight down the main road off our residential streets. One time, it was in the evening, when we had finished our class, a car pulled up with a few boys in it. Apparently my friend knew one of them from where she worked. In the back was his brother who turned out to be my flame (you). I was somehow then sitting in the back with you.

North Rd Oakleigh 1963

At some point after my Running I would become devastated at the loss of the love of my life. Why, oh why, could I not have been more advanced and awake earlier in my life? Well, the answer to that is that if we were already awake we wouldn't be here in our current lifetimes to work through healing our past traumas.

This is about 'awakening' and 'atonement'
We were not even adults when we met. That was part of the magic — that simple innocence was joyful and fulfilling. We spent 5 years together dating and going places, dancing, swimming, watching the big live bands and going to the drive-ins and other movies.

We then married. It was once again a magic day. We had kept from indulging in the fires of passion for that special day. It was a day that I would wish could last forever and not end.

So many life pleasures lay in store for us but we didn't see the problems or the pain of life. We were blind to what life can secretly have in store. The pleasures of our relationship, the pleasures of life together, the opportunities to open up to these things — we just did not see.

Memories flood me: The two of us at the front porch of my Mum's house. We spent time there after returning from many nights out or in the kitchen. That's how we indulged our passions back then. Kissing and cuddling for a long time.

So often, I see that picture in my mind and it's in full colour. It's alive. I feel those feelings and smell the perfume of the night.

On that front porch, he reached his hand behind my neck, touching gently my soft, cool, white, but feverish skin. Our lips met and caused an electrical shock, reverberating out from us and changing and blending our auras into one. This sealed our connection into infinity and beyond even that.

Also driving to Sorrento to spend a day at the beach. Driving regularly to your parents' country town shop. We always stayed for the weekend.

The music that was us and our life — The Shadows, The Kinks and The Beatles. The first record you gave me – Cliff Richard's 'Constantly'. Going out to live band shows. There were many of them back then. Great memories of that time and the places we went and the bands we saw and danced to dreamily.

We went ten pin bowling. There was also the photo booth at the same venue where we took crazy photos. I remember them easily but no longer have them. They got lost over the years. I don't have a lot of photos from that era. We were obviously too engrossed in our joyful life to bother taking many.

We were 'The Innocents' back then

In many ways we still are
Those Innocents deserve their forever-after time

When we were first married and living in our new house — those beautiful evenings where we would sit in the lounge room and you would brush my very long hair. Other times you would wash my hair for me in the bathroom basin. I love these memories — they are sweet and delightful.

They touch my heart today. I am forever remembering our days in the sun. We can bring back the sun and it can burn forever for us. That sun will shine on our faces and shoulders and warm us again.

Then after the difficulties of our first pregnancy and the difficult birth of our first daughter — that time when she was ten months old — we went with your mum to take her for her first swimming lesson. It was very unusual in that era to take a baby to swimming lessons. She was later to be a competition swimmer.

We were matched, just like the mirror images of Twin Flames. We thought the same and had the same views of everything we did together. We did not argue. We loved the same activities. We both had great respect also for each other. Many years down the track I would ask myself "where, oh where, is my true love" and "why, oh why, did I run?". I had no answers or perception back then that it was all part of the 'Twin Flame' story — the break and separation — the realisation — and the chasing and seeking back.

All divinely orchestrated. Even though we both suffered much pain and the illusion of loss I am very grateful for all we've now been through and how it all led us back to our more passionate reunion. If all the pain did not occur then we would not be back together again.

This book is You and this book is Me
It's only words
But words are what will bring you back to me

~~~

Take me beyond this world

Far from the restraints

of time, place or borders

...

Where fear does not exist

Where only our love can be

...

CHAPTER 22

Our Memories: 1963-1982+
– Angel –

*T*he Memories will fill our minds with joy and also with the energies that keep us joined. They are tangible 'things' that exist in all dimensions of time and space. The memories spin in the vortex that is our love.

They spin in my mind and in my soul. I connect to them frequently now because I'm in the awakened stage. The stage where I know the truth and feel our reunion coming closer.

Please remember what I discovered by doing past trauma healing work on myself. We spent quite a few years — around 6 years plus — in a separation split mode.

I realised later that's when I felt lost and that I had lost your true love connection to me. That is the reason for my 'Running Away'. It was never because I met someone else as everyone thought at the time. No, it was never that. I was waiting for you all that time to reconnect to me but I should have initiated it myself. I should have pushed the right buttons.

I thought, completely wrongly, that I had now found love. But in reality I had left it behind. My twin flame and I are unable to ever be separated in truth. It can't be done. The illusions took over my life during this separation. I'm very thankful I learnt much and that I then awoke.

I mistakenly thought that this second relationship I went into was real. It was an illusion like all other intrusions into our own true love flame relationship. It did not last long before I knew this. But I was again stuck in my own lack of confidence and thought I could never have another split. I thought it would break me.

The only thing that ever broke me was separation from you. That separation pain went on and on for me. That separation time was also our saviour.

It is now just up to us both to realise all of this. Let no-one make any judgements or decisions about us. We belong to you and me.

Knight: Please know this: Life could never have been beautiful without you. Let's look at all our paranormal situations that, at the time, we thought of as simply normal. We were together in the land of forever. It was home.

1963 Angel met Knight: The love of my life, at that age. I've never stopped loving you. I was 16 and you had just turned 17. That age I would love to live through always again and again. We both will live through it always and ever, again and again.

I went through a terrible time during later lost years when I would also wake in the night in terror. I couldn't understand this terror. It seemed to be a terror of living. I sometimes got up in the night and had a shower and in the bathroom I looked in the mirror and saw a terrified face. It was out of my control. I'm not sure what you, my Twin Flame (mate), thought or whether I even said much about it to you. I'm absolutely sure you did not understand any of it at all. I only understand it myself now — in the present time. But you still supported me.

I remember thinking while showering in the middle of the night one time — that I needed you to hold me till the fear in me subsided. But somehow I was unaware of how to ask this. I can now see clearly how that terrible time contributed to our eventual (temporary) split.

I'm now sure that this was the first 'break' in our relationship even though I didn't realise it at the time. If our former closeness and connection was still in the forefront then I probably would not have felt disconnected. But at the same time it's more than possible that my disconnection from myself and life was the catalyst for our final breakup. These incidences of ill-health had set us up for our journey of life. I wish sometimes I could go back and change all that. But of course life is all about going through the dark to get to the light.

What, I now think to myself, causes these night fears to erupt? Are they life traumas? Are they simply life itself that a mere over-sensitive soul cannot tolerate? It was not just me that went through these life challenges but I'm aware that you also went through your own fair share.

We were far too unknowledgeable to join together to heal those traumas. Instead we allowed them to split us apart. Both of us feeling the pain and separation and what we thought of as 'lack of love'. Both of us were retreating and running instead of healing the hurt together by going through the dark to arrive at light.

I learnt that years ago during another challenge in my life. I was climbing a mountain. Yes, that's exactly what I was doing on a health retreat. I was afraid of heights but I pushed on up that mountain. There was no track as such, just chains in some of the higher parts. I made it.

But … then when it was time to go back down I simply could not face it. Going down is worse when you are afraid of heights. That is the time that I pushed through my fears and went through it instead. I decided there was no other choice so I literally flew down that mountain looking out into the light and also looking below me. My fear vanished. I've never forgotten that lesson in life.

It wasn't just random that I decided to push through that fearful time. I decided to focus on the one thing that had been increasingly sustaining me since I had already started on my spiritual journey. I focused on my mentor and the light. Whenever there seems to be an obstacle, then choose to go through it and don't run away or try to avoid it.

It is definitely possible to change the future and destiny. We chose our lives together to learn and eventually be reunited with new insight and understanding and with more powerful fire and passion. This was all in our destiny.

Remember The Real People: Yes, it is always the two real people I remember. It's not those two foolish people (the illusions) who existed during our relationship decline and split. Those two don't exist anymore. I have healed on many emotional levels since then. You have also.

There is purpose to the split and reunion. We still love those people we were as teenagers and for many years after that. Just as we love those two people we have become and who will reunite now. We just don't relate to the two Twin Flame lovers who broke apart and forgot who they were. Just like at birth, we fell into forgetfulness for a while.

Pure Memories Seemed To Be Lost: I lost sight of the pure memories for a while — because I focussed on my current illusory pain and fear of loss. A lot was covered up by chronic illness and pain. If you lose sight of your love then your body reacts and becomes ill. Our physical hearts both broke.

It was as simple as that. I lost sight. Fear of loss can cause the appearance of actual loss. Now I've gained my insight back I have to reunite with the true love of my life. This is You, my Twin.

It works both ways. When I visualise and actually see us together and reunited then the universe connects to us and manifests the actual joining back together. It can't fail.

~ ~ ~

You Have Returned To Me
My True Love

...

Because You Never
Really Left Me

...

It's My Sweet Surrender

&

I'm totally lost in you

...

The Golden Rings

CHAPTER 23

The Breaking: 1986-1992
– Angel –

A fter many years of love, family and learning, the breaking began. We were never prepared for what was to come. Still innocents. Our love still joined forever.

Our connection seemed to fade away and we both looked with fear at who we were and what our lives had become.

All this had already been preordained and told to us while we were in the pre-1946 time, travelling in the paranormal dimensions. With each of our births we were clouded and veiled from the truth. We had forgotten our travels before birth.

While going through chronic illness about 1975 I, Angel, called out to Knight on the etheric level: "Knight please save me from this illness that takes me away from our path and from you." He did not hear this. He was in forgetfulness and veiled from hearing me. There were many stresses that broke this beautiful family. None of us are prepared in advance for these things. All the more reason why, when we are taken by surprise, we cannot deal with it all and we allow ourselves to weaken.

Everything was good for a while — quite a few years. Two daughters were born. One was first to become a victim of anxiety and become sleepless after starting school. By then a third daughter had been born and she succumbed to allergies, asthma and skin problems. When daughter number four was born she was happy and healthy. By that time both of us, Angel and Knight, had also been through illnesses that required sudden surgery.

Was it any wonder we were strained and our minds and hearts had been parted for a number of years. We were struggling to survive, each of us separately instead of together.

Larger struggles were to come, so we grew further apart. This could never have been even imagined at our very start when life was beautiful all the time.

We all have our vortexes but life causes many of them to change when we do. The wrong colours and energies. That's when our traumas come out to affect us and we falter on our life path. Somehow we strayed into different vortexes and lost each other. By 1990 I had found new interests that took me away from home a number of times a week. I could not see what was happening. I felt an energy pull that would take me away from Knight. I failed to recognise how painful this would be and how it just should not be happening. That pull was very strong.

I thought Knight had left me mentally and in his heart. It definitely looked that way on the surface and my heart pained me. I felt it deeply. My view of the world was then taken away and I saw someone else I imagined was my answer to a new life of love and ease. This was to be my major error and my learning a lot the hard way. It was not visible that this new person had a huge flaw I would not cope with.

Would I have stayed? Stayed with that interloper, the second marriage, if he had not become so cold and showed his major psychological problems to me? Would I have remained fooled and not woken up to my true love?

Sometimes I reflect on this horrid possibility. Mostly I manage to clear all those thoughts away. I know fully now that only thinking about all the good in my life and the creations I am participating in is the solution through to living the life we chose together. I am also completely aware that both myself and Knight are living examples of our pre-ordained destinies. Our destiny is true love that no-one can ever intervene in.

I also know that pushing those dark thoughts down and hiding them is a danger also. They must be brought out into the open, surrounded by love and then allowed to fade and evaporate completely. This way they are gone from our lives forever. I still sometimes think of all those years without Knight. How was I ever so foolish? We needed each other so many times but the rest of our lifetimes we will now have left together will make up for this many times over. Because the entire pact is a whole. None of it is in pieces. It all fits into the tapestry of our lives that was already pacted and agreed to.

"I'm kicking myself," I say to Knight: "That I didn't tell you over 20 years ago. I could have. I seemed to have lacked the courage then. My courage currently is hitting the roof or even the clouds — therefore there is nothing I won't do for you or to return you to your rightful place."

It is the way of humans. They still mostly have not learnt. It takes a lifetime for most to learn how to live. I look now at all of humanity and feel great pain and pity for them. They know not what they are doing. The rich live for the moment and the powerful create wars and harm many. "Knight, we can contribute to the healing of many people on this Earth now. It is a gift given to us that we have awakened to everything available to us."

I knew that this second marriage somehow made me feel it should be true love (as I am a Pisces) and this false thought is what took me from my true love. Everything challenging the two young lovers, the young marrieds, the new parents and later the full time work kept the real lovers apart.

My second marriage means now we, the older, retired, NOT matched pair have all day to spend together but love doesn't exist here in our house together. I could find myself lost and alone and crying nearly every day. Where is the true love life I should be living and loving with you, Knight, each and every day? Where is our joy? I am lost. I will always be lost without you — because you are the other half of me.

I had many years to realise I had lost you Knight and why. I became aware of the spell and our pathway in life. Also I am aware of why it was happening. It still took me quite some time to accept the hardships of my current life that I seemed to have chosen and the knowing and accepting of the faith and knowledge that it would all change as soon as the spell manifested it and as soon as we accepted our fate together. Any spell must be believed in to do its work with the utmost power. All this pain and loneliness will pass — as all things must pass.

Back then, after the breaking, believe it or not Knight

— I cried a river for two whole years.

Also I cried many times after that.

~~~

Dear Flame ...

Do You Know How Much

We Really Are To

Each Other ...

CHAPTER 24

The Changes: 1992-2023

*E*ach day the changing began. Angel had allowed her heart and mind to be directed to a new life. She chose to run away with someone else thinking her children would also go with her. She had made a huge error in estimating what she was doing. For the next 30 years she would cry more than she ever had in her entire life before so far. For 2 years she missed her children. It looked to the world like she had abandoned them.

But her heart was broken. New relationships and even two marriages occurred, with them. For Knight, one short relationship and then a marriage — and both were not meant to be more than learning experiences. He suffered in both these relationships. Far more than Angel ever realised.

A marriage for her, Angel, that she was fooled into thinking was some kind of saviour event and that it would last and that she would now be happy. That was foolish thinking. She was being led to learning and her life path but she had no idea it would be so painful. She also suffered greatly during this time. While, unbeknown to her, Knight was also suffering. Eventually she came to believe she had been led to her execution. More and more as time went by.

From the start they both had trouble with these new partners. We had forgotten how to go back to the purple dimension where we made our pact. We remained puzzled by all that was going on around us. Knight tried quite a few times to get her back with him. Why did she not go? This she would wonder. Even though she knows it. They would still have had problems, they would not have had the learning and their passion may not have been released as it now is.

Knight was lucky to escape those first relationships that were doing him wrong and the marriage. The thing is, if Angel had known his first marriage failed fairly quickly then she would have made a move towards him and many years would not have been wasted. Even though when she looks through the cards she was dealt in her so-called new life — she realises she had a lot to learn. Even though also her anger and resentment at her situation was hard to keep in check. It was mostly directed at herself. Her need to become calm and accepting is now crucial and bringing about changes in her physical world.

Sensual Memories: Angel's thoughts: "I remember your touch — so soft on my hair — and the way that you whispered 'baby be at peace now'. I remember your care and protection and that feeling of so being loved. I miss you more than I can ever say."

"But, believe me, I will definitely be saying all of this to you very, very soon in the Now time. At that moment everything will change for many people but mostly for us. I remember also your scent. It is special and evokes feelings in me that will never be gone."

Changes: Day by day changes are occurring. Angel knows how to handle the coming of the new life they have been promised together. She is fully aware not to force any issues. She has been told this before birth. As time goes by and she learns more and more about how to get to the reunion and the life changes, she still does get impatient — but never will she force any action. The manifesting simply will not work from force. It never will. It's something important for many people in the world to learn about manifesting. Many times they try it but they don't understand it. Angel does understand all the issues and ideals behind manifesting.

The Premonition Vision: This premonition vision appeared to them both during a time of their marriage when Knight was seriously ill. It was very much early in their marriage when they had not yet had any children.

Out of nowhere there appeared before them an explosion of light with many beams of various shades of blue and purple. Stars were also splashed throughout these beams. Knight was thrust into this light burst. Looking fearful he held out his hand to Angel. She reached out spontaneously to grab him.

She also was fearful and tried to bring him back. She ended up spinning into that burst of colour and light. She could still not reach him and she became aware that she was not meant to.

He was still trying to reach his hand out to her. Something unknown to them was stopping her from saving him, even though she was aware that this was her mission in this phenomenon.

Because they both were in a dark energy space in their minds, they did not think clearly or ask for the light to help them. They were still not awakened to that way through challenges. Nothing like this had happened to them before in their lives so both were astounded by it all.

He then disappeared momentarily and she felt lost. This all happened so quickly that suddenly it was over. This was the premonition of what was to come for them both.

Then suddenly they were back in their own house and she was calling the emergency number. They came and took him to hospital. She became aware that this had been a premonition but she was unsure of its true meaning. Unknown to her it was a warning that their various illnesses and emergencies in their future life would eventually threaten to separate them. They were being shown to save each other. A warning of events to come for them in the future.

They had always tried to support and save each other to the best of their abilities but at some point it would no longer work for them. All along they were made to be unaware of their before life pact and the spell. They were purposely working through life in the dark. On purpose with their chosen destiny together.

They became exhausted and worn down by life and things just began to wear out. The signs did come for them. Whenever these signs show up in the Now time Angel recognised them now. She can heed them and move forward. That ability comes from the long learning. Anyone can see it is all worth it eventually. The only reason she is now seeming to be far more in love and passionate about them, and only them, has nothing to do with being with someone else unsuitable for a while.

There was nothing to learn about loving Knight there in the failed second marriage, except what she learnt naturally from being deprived of him for such a long time. From missing Knight! She also learnt about compassion with this second marriage, even when the person you are caring for is no longer connected to you.

~~~

The Golden Rings

PART THREE:

The Love and Passion

The Golden Rings

CHAPTER 25

The Turning: 1997-2023
– Angel –

*D*ay *by day* the turning began. I was gradually awakening. I know that you, Knight, were always seeking me out in the early years. Then you eventually went into hiding and none of us knew where you were or what you were feeling. My intuition of you is extensive and I realised later how hurt you were. Hurting makes people run away. I'm sorry it took me so long.

How many times later did I wish I had accepted you when you sought me out? That pact we designed way back pre-1946 means each of the two of us must awaken to it separately. It was to be one by one. It took me too long to wake up and when I did you had closed your eyes once again.

You Were Sleeping: I now have to wake you one more time Sleeping Beauty. These vows were taken before we both were born.

We have to remember that and be accepting of things right now. We wait and we are rewarded with our new, but never really broken, relationship. The fire will burn in our hearts. The pact steered us into the abyss of being apart for that long. Our awakenings had to be only facilitated in the fullness of time. It could take a long time or perhaps not.

I'm aware we both agreed to this pact and spell and with joy. We felt brave then before we were born. In Earth life right now 2023 I feel sad and weak. I just want it finished. I desire the love back.

I have now turned completely. Everything in between, after the split, and now, the reunion is just part of our learning path and the path that leads not only us but entire families to atonement and forgiveness. There will be many celebrations for this on Earth.

The spiritual realms will celebrate at the same time as we do. Peace will reign in the dimension we came from and also here on Earth. It will be a matching of above and below. We agreed to participate in this event long ago.

If we stand hand-in-hand in front of a brilliant sunset in the evening we will feel the sun's rays light the flame. It will draw us through into our new realm.

Although it pains me, I have to accept that if we had rejoined years back before the completion of our awakenings, then we would have lost the opportunity to rejoin with the utmost ecstasy and passion.

"This Reunion, that is pacted and pre-ordained, still cannot take place unless you wake up, Knight," says Angel softly to herself. He had to go through the dark forest of deathly shadows first. If Angel had been fully awakened years and years ago he would have awakened then if she approached him. It was not to be that easy way. They have both agreed long ago to making their path difficult for them so as to have the greatest learning and the greatest advancement.

If I could love anyone in the world, it would still be you. If you had not been born into this lifetime, then I would not have existed. I wondered how long you had been on my mind ... then I realised, since long before we were born into this life, because Twin Flames are the One Soul.

People Are Nudging Me

This is unknown even to us. For instance, my sister has taken to giving me gifts from my past.

Books, a bear (exactly as one that my kids had in the 1980s) and even more shock making — some canisters that are exactly the ones we had for our kitchen in the 1970s. They could even have been the very same ones. A huge reminder of the happy times together. I am keeping these for the new home we will share together.

Another friend gave me information that is vital for me to know about our true relationship. It's all falling into place. I, Angel, easily may have stalled in my quest if I had not heard this unrequested information.

This friend spoke the words. Words will bring us back together.

I used to worry about the outcome

Would we or would we not reunite? I often despaired of this. But I have learnt the way of the law of attraction and felt the spell I am under now. I now know that it can never not happen. Nothing in the universe can stop it now. If I were to continue to stress and have outbursts about whether or not it will happen and fearing that it may not, then I can now see that I would actually be stopping the flow of the manifesting. It now is all about to manifest on this Earth plane.

"I hear the sound of your breath
I feel your love in my being"
– by Angel

~~~

Spiritual and Emotional

Cords Still Bind Us

In Pure Love

...

The Truth Is ...

They Can't Be Broken

The Golden Rings

CHAPTER 26

Twin Hearts: 2008-2020

*D*uring *this period the twin hearts* physically broke down. Both Twin Flames' hearts finally broke and needed mending at this time. The toll was too much on both of them. First for Knight his heart 'exploded' and almost killed him. He was saved by fate. This could not occur and the twin flames miss their destiny of reuniting. So he has been put back together quite a few times and his heart currently is on hold for Angel. Still ticking over well.

Then we reach 2020 and Angel's heart almost gave out. It was not in quite the spectacular way as Knight's. In fact, with Angel, it was a silent breaking down. As is her nature in Pisces she remains silent when she should possibly be shouting. Once again it was only the fate of the spell that gave her the insight to seek out tests that showed she needed urgent repair on her heart. There was no real warning this was coming for her but when Knight had no warning it meant it was sudden and almost fatal.

Over all this time apart they were still in sync. Their hearts were both broken. But hearts can be repaired, especially if the owners of them are participating in a pact that absolutely must be followed through on.

At this time, while they are seemingly in limbo waiting for their reunion and their healing, neither heart has been perfectly repaired yet. Neither on the physical level or the etheric level.

It will take the manifestation of the actual reunion and the spreading out of the love to repair them completely. They will both suddenly have far more energy and the blood will circulate around their bodies from their hearts so much more efficiently. They will have been given extra time on Earth by the spell if they have woken up and returned to each other. They can be gifted up to 10 more years or even beyond that.

Their own precious family will all be mended at this time as well. There have been fractures along the way because the twin hearts split apart.

This family and the splits in them have been the sorrow of Angel for many years. Her tears have often flowed for them all.

~~~

Any partners we turned to in the past or at the present time

...

They will fade

Our Light will dim them

...

The Golden Rings

CHAPTER 27

Eternal Memories
– Angel –

*A*ll our Memories fill us with love and light and that other special feeling that is hard to explain. It's not easy to put your finger on it. It's a connection and an enjoyment spanning many years. "Knight, I can access them very easily now and they bring a glow to both of us when I share with you." Knight responds to me: "Angel, you are truly my angel. You glow with the memories of us." I know already we will now make new memories when we have rejoined.

"Our memories don't just start from 1963 but they start from way before 1946. When we were in the purple dimensions. When we were starting out and making the pact with the guides. Before we were born," said Knight, whispering softly to me in our future. Knight will then recognise the part The Golden Rings played in all of this. "Let us fulfil the destiny of The Golden Rings. Let us purchase the new ring and inscribe it," he will say to me with utter conviction when he is awake and ready.

He will be completely enthusiastic about doing this more than ever after our reunion.

This new ring obviously signifies a new marriage. We can wipe out the memories from around 1982 until 1992. Or fade them. They weren't very special good memories then. They were the start of our parting.

We will be making new ones now. Filled with love, connection and doing everything together, holding hands and gazing into each others' eyes. All this will start the vibrations all around us. Flowers, bees, trees, rivers and the ocean will all vibrate now.

We will travel and see things with new eyes. The rest of our lives here on Earth will be filled with everything we neglected to do together during the Split time.

Let our love wipe out those years and times we thought we were not connected. We were under a spell. The pact we signed that steered our Destiny here caused us to forget for the purpose of living out the prophecies imparted to us.

If none of that had occurred then the fierce desire and passion we are connected by would never have been fired up. We can't just exist but must live. We would have remained innocent, slow, quiet and non assuming. How would we ever have accessed all the love we all along deserved?

But now the passion will be let free. It will be wild and wonderful now.

We will dance as we did all those years ago. It was one of the 'car shows' you loved to organise. We danced, we laughed, we loved and we ran. We ran so far we barely remembered our way back.

This was during the beginning of the turning. We were both touched by 'The Golden Rings' spell that was on us. It dropped our egos off way back in time. This was the time of movement and joy.

Suddenly we stopped and I looked into your beautiful eyes. Those eyes I knew so well. They returned the love to me and we swam in a pool of light and love. It supported us and we could never drown in it. We could only be surrounded and filled by it.

Although we were always under the spell of The Golden Rings and other pacts — we were also cursed at the time of our split and breakup. We would remain cursed until it was broken. There was always a secret act for it to be broken. We had both forgotten what this was. It was hidden from us all those years. We were meant to have forgotten because when this act occurred without us being aware — well that's the secret and then it all falls into place.

Well, as I (Angel) have awoken first and fully, I now 'know' what this secret act is. It is something I have only very recently learnt of. I can organise this to occur, but ... can I really and truly pull this off? It will take great courage for me to instigate it.

It's not an act that only one person can do and then magic happens. No ... no ... no ... it has to be acted on by the two people simultaneously. There must be action and also reaction.

Is it possible that I can participate in this act spontaneously? Not really if I know about it. It would need to be planned and may not work for that reason.

Kiss the Knight
Break the Spell

Spellbound

Yes, we've been spellbound for many, many years. If we look back it can cause distress. It is best to see each other only in the Now but with the realisation that we would not be who we are in the Now unless we had our very long Past to have brought it all about.

We can only ever look back at the sweet memories. Our first times of everything. Our teenage years were incredibly special. We can bring that magic to our Now time and never let it go.

Any disagreements mean absolutely nothing now. Why did we ever bother to stress over them and cause any arguments? Who cares now? When that spell is broken it will all fall away. It will dissolve.

~~~

It is now written
Indelibly on the universal field

...

We are reuniting, rejoining and
reigniting

...

Any partners we turned to in the
past or at the present time

...

They are disappearing

CHAPTER 28

Sudden Changes: 1992-2023
– Angel –

*E*ventually *the critical change day* arrives. Although it seems to appear suddenly, in actual fact it has been a long time coming. Many years have gone into the gradual learning and the changes.

You could say, even from that fateful day the Split began, that awakening has been an undercurrent all along. Hard to imagine this if we look back at events. But it's still true.

For six years we had not made love. It was painful. We were both hurt but neither could see the other's pain. So it actually all started in 1986. Whenever I, Angel, was not caring for our children or our house I did my own thing now.

Art, creative things, house decorating, courses or part time jobs. I also spent time at shopping centres or cafes, having a coffee alone and missing the biggest part of my life — my Twin Flame.

I missed our togetherness and our love to the point that it was so painful.

One day I came upon another soul who also seemed lost to the world he lived in. This brought us a friendship that went on for two years. There was nothing romantic or untoward about this friendship. He spoke of losing contact with his own family and wife. They still lived together but never spoke.

I, being a Pisces, was instantly concerned and felt his pain also. It seemed to mirror my own. This was the start of the illusion created by destiny to catch us all in the play of life. It was about the forgiveness and atonement now. A situation had to be created by our spiritual guides to enable a painful split that would go on for years and then be healed by the reunion. I now had lost sight completely of Knight. How could this ever be?

Eventually it came to a head. Suddenly once day something snapped. We went out together and connected. We were so unhappy that we decided to run away together. This was so out of character — particularly for Angel, myself. I had no real insight as to how this would work.

I day-dreamed and imagined that my children would be better off away from arguments at home. Another foolish illusion that took my attention away from reality and real love. It only meant we would all lose you for years.

I was in for a shock when these two lost souls eventually ran away. My children were shocked and would not go with me as I had thought they would. This is not an outcome

I would ever have thought would occur way back in the 60s. Knight was the love of my life. Without me realising of course, he was my Twin Flame too.

I would never go on to survive long without him. It could never be a forever split. We would wake up and it would all be mended. Just staying with the faith would ensure everything.

But the destinies had been pacted already before our birth. There would inevitably be a split, a running, a chasing and a long chasm of the unique loneliness that comes only with a Twin Flame break.

I was now missing my children and somehow wished this had never happened. Knight became my Chaser — I was the Runner. Now, in the present time, 2023 how I wished I had run home to Knight.

In this time of Now I can't even imagine the way of my thinking back then. It was not part of me. Although Knight seemed to disappear from our lives for quite some years — there came a time when he came back. He instigated a return to his family. He made overtures to his children. He had realised what had been lost by him closing off from them. I myself was moved by this. True inner feelings were stirred.

I made every effort from that time onwards to be where Knight was and go to places where I knew he would be. I didn't even admit to myself what I was doing but whenever we were at the same place I felt the comfort of being closer to him.

I am unsure whether he noticed this phenomenon or not. I think back now and wonder why I did not make a move back then when it would have been so much easier. I was just stuck in a pattern. Clearly a pattern made by the spell.

~~~

And Let It Be

Like We Said It Would Be

...

You'll Always Be The One

...

The Golden Rings

CHAPTER 29

Awakening: 2018-2023

This is the time when Angel waits and waits. She has already awakened even though it took her so very long. He got tired of waiting and he feared being alone. He had found someone else. He already knew this new person would never replace Angel.

"I can be happy now," said Knight in his illusions. His partner suited him but was not prepared to live only for him daily. He decided to be prepared to be happy with this situation. He is still unaware that Angel can come to him at any moment and change everything in his current life.

She is completely ready now for the atonement. She will fix every single life problem he has or ever did have. Just by being there with him and living the life of love and devotion daily.

We started in the spring — then spring became summer. It was 1963. 'How would she have believed he would have come along back then' They were touching hands and reaching out. They were innocent at that beginning spring time. They were combined/ attached instantly. This cannot ever be broken. All it takes now is for Knight to become fully awakened. He was once aware only of her and her love but he didn't have the skills to show this to her in those formative innocent years. Passion that smouldered beneath the surface all along was pushed down simply by lack of knowledge.

When Angel ran away because she imagined she had lost your love, Knight — she was running from lost love not to new love. There was never any new love at all. It was all illusion.

"I'm not giving up on you, Knight" said Angel with a passion. "And you won't be giving up on me when you wake up and realise our entire story."

"Knight, Knight! Our energy is overpowering me now. I feel you every day. You are with me, you are within me, you are me." Angel speaks out loud. As she does to Knight now everyday.

The spoken out loud word carries easier into the universal field. All their prayers, hopes and desires are now out there in the field. The words are indelibly written forever. They can't ever be erased. The words now will be manifested by universal law.

It is now back in March of 2022 (that year of happenings). Angel has had a meeting with a very good friend of hers. She is also a mutual friend of both Angel and Knight. She once again uttered magic words that are direct messages from the Angels 11:11.

The words once again tell her a story. "Knight loves me still," thought Angel immediately. There was no mistake in the words told to her. They were direct. Angel could not miss their meaning. Those words said to her clearly that she is still the love of his life. It's all she needs.

Although this chapter is dated 2018-2023 Angel actually started to awaken by as far back as 1997. She felt powerless to do anything then but it took all those years to realise that she actually could change everything for both of them. To realise that she actually had that strength because it got stronger and stronger.

2018-2023 refers to the time when she was most active in her creating of change and returning to her true love. Also when she knew the old was dead.

By this time she had fully awakened not only to their Twin Flame connection and pact but also to the fact that she had power. The intuitive messages kept coming now, fast and strong. She absolutely knew what to do now.

Knight is still acting like he hasn't yet awakened or turned. But this is an act to save him from perceived sorrow. Angel now understands his lack of action. He was hurt once and doesn't want that again so he pretends not to be interested. It's now obvious.

This friend of Angel's at a meeting about the same time the previous year also spoke words of wonder to Angel. Angel was shocked and did not expect to hear these words. They were words directly from Knight's mouth this friend told her. She had never asked any questions that would lead to this information.

So, now with both times, words like these, they should be spoken directly to Angel. When will he get the courage for this? The spell of The Golden Rings and the before birth pact will always be more powerful than Knight. They will win him over to soon make his turning. Now that Angel knows about the words (the messages) that he has spoken, she also knows she still has to act on the advice of her guardians.

She still has jobs to do but they are not as arduous as she had imagined. Not long to go now. It's all happening. She took the golden shining advice, followed it all through, and now she sees that everything is manifesting. Just like 'The Law of Attraction' promises us all. Be faithful, be grateful and learn to be patient. If everyone follows this they will see the fruit of their deepest desires come true.

"It's only maybe months away now. We will make an announcement when the change occurs. Tell the World," they have thought these simultaneous thoughts all at once now — "We have decided to be happy every single day of the rest of our lives now."

"It matters not who likes or does not like this — the world is ours and our own world is within us only forever now," says Knight.

"Dearest, my love, we will repair and heal every single person in our vicinity or in our lives. Just first, Knight, let us heal our own hearts. They broke, our breast skin was cut open down the centre, then our sternum bone sawed through so that our hearts could be mended physically. Our entire system was shut down and a machine took over for us," responds Angel.

That is the optimal time when your spiritual guardians can make contact with your subconscious minds. The time when your physical bodies and hearts are cut off from your physical lives and consciousness, they were told.

When they woke up from this unconsciousness they would not remember what information they were given.

It's up to them now to mend their spiritual hearts, their One Soul and everything else. They have within their subconscious minds what was told to them while their hearts were turned off and disconnected from their bodies.

It's all in their hands now as they have been reminded of the pact and the spell. They both went through a dizzying time when their chests were sewn up and they awoke.

Even though they couldn't remember what they had been told it still sat alive in their minds.

~~~

We need to recognise the pact and everlasting love

...

That our love was always there

*It never left ...
We just had to see it*

CHAPTER 30

Pending Reunion: 2019-2023
– Angel –

*T*his is the moment we have waited for. I have had that epiphany moment in time when I recognised the truth. Everything has come together all at once after the initial parting. It started many years ago. I, Angel, was having thoughts of reconnection and of past realities. I was becoming 'knowing' of how things really were. I was slow at first. Only finding myself looking forward to glimpses of Knight, my flame.

Not even recognising what a Twin Flame relationship even was during that early stage of 2019. But the angels awakening me do not need to work super fast in these cases.

I was, by now, learning all things spiritual in my life. I had been having psychic experiences since the end of the year 2000. This was the time my mother passed away and it was instant after that day. The day of her passing was the guiding light to me. My awakening was accelerated from that very day onwards. I awoke to the truths of life and death and that we are all never-ending.

But, all this drifting apart and losing each other was preordained. We will both recognise this at our reunion or very soon after it is completed. It was our gift to others. Many will be healed through us.

It is of course a clique and has been said many times before, but I can never settle for anyone who is not The One.

"All those who meet their 'One' will know what this means, Knight." But it really only occurs for Twin Flames.

I stand here now waiting for you because of the Scent you have left with me. It fills me now. That Scent from all those early years ago that can never leave me ever.

He will surely respond with a deep passionate kiss. "If ever there was The One for me it can be no-one else but you," will be his murmurings.

He has learnt a thing or two over the years. All those years being with the wrong one because he didn't want to be alone. It was really because he missed Angel so, so much.

In the year 2022 he has also finally kissed the ring. This sets in motion the future scenes relating to the spell and the pact. We will also travel to where the other original ring was 'lost'. It's clearly not likely we will ever find it, and maybe years ago someone else did find it. But we probably won't be advertising for it. It can absolutely never belong to anyone else and it may even process a wrong spell onto them if they keep it thinking it is theirs now.

The pact meant we were to buy another and have it made exactly as a copy and it was to become part of the spell. That action is part of the spell for a reason. That reason is that if the Twin Flames are moved enough to purchase a complete new copy of the original ring then we have declared our love as bigger than we could ever have imagined.

"Knight I am so sorry at the time we did not look further and now feel the pain of the loss of the ring. Obviously it was part of our imagining we had lost our love to not show care about the ring then."

It fell into a lake of brown water while he was swimming and it was not known exactly where. It was as if it was not to be found by us at all. This is the truth of the pact.

I have now got the pearl headband and the magic pearls for our new wedding. The pearls have been mended professionally and, of course, they come from my parents and were given to me for my 21st birthday. They were worn for our first wedding at the church we love in Oakleigh.

You know, the only things needed for our wedding now are the pearl ear-rings, the making of the silk wedding dress, the finishing of the pink silk dress for our going away and our family and friends wedding party to come after the secret wedding and honeymoon.

The rejoicing will ring out into the universe then. Our amazing and spiritually strong four girls are going to be healed with this wedding and rejoining of their family with love. These four girls have had their crying times.

I promise you this:
No matter who enters your life
… for whatever reason
I will still love you more
than anyone else ever could

I will tell him: "I want to hold your hand, laugh everyday, walk with you, snuggle together to talk about anything and everything, gaze into your eyes and kiss your lips every single day of our lives together. It's been too long without all of this."

"We will talk forever about our first loves and those first loves we talk about will be each other." What changes shall we see? Yes, we've been through the path and the challenges and we have changed and learnt a lot. But — the soul does not change, it simply experiences. Ours have not changed from before we came here as Twin Flames.

We can adjust to the new people we are on the human level because the basis of our incarnation and existence has not changed.

The spell could not touch that. A message for everyone reading this book: 'You have chosen this life, so now you must live it.'

Just Before The Reunion

The time is approaching very soon and it is very much unsettling for many in the family but especially for us, the lovers. So long apart and now the time and the very essence of how we think is changing quickly. Knight has been going into a depression for a few years now. One of the extra factors in this is the loss of his best friend, his pet dog.

This depression is not like him at all. But he is alone still and doesn't want to be. Is he still unaware of all the love that's coming and his new life? Yes, clearly he can't feel those true emotions yet — they do not fill his entire being as they do with me, Angel. If only I could let him know it all. Very soon I can do just that. I will soon be lying in your arms and you will gaze at me because I will be your 'bird of paradise'.

"That day is drawing so near now," I say in my daily dream musings, "that I can almost name the day and date." So far, in all these years, he has not found the right partner that takes his entire love and matches him. Angel also has not found this. No-one else fills their lives. It is not even possible.

Well, of course, they are not meant to. This will never happen for either of them in this lifetime because still relatively unknown to him but known to me, we are Twin Flames and forever we are One.

I have been made aware of his depression and I am feeling sadness and the tears behind my eyes for him. I know I could fix this immediately — if only it was the right time and space. Because the timing is not right yet I cannot run to him and heal him yet. But it's not long to wait now.

The spell will not allow any of the timings to be broken. That would mean the entire pact would not work for all those concerned. When you make a pact with your spiritual guides for the best for all concerned then you simply cannot break it.

Strong energies will hold back on anyone trying to break a pact or spell. Souls who incarnate as mere humans do not have the inner power to be able to do this. A spiritual spell has power far beyond any human.

~~~

*The Reunion signals
reverberations out
into the infinite
universe*

...

*It is now written indelibly
on the Universal Field
for manifestation*

...

The Golden Rings

CHAPTER 31

Awake Now: 2019-2023

he is growing and curling her hair, regaining her health and fitness, fixing her teeth and throwing away old items that no longer fit into their new life together — revamping and renewing all the surrounding energies. She is getting ready for the explosive reunion. She is now wide awake to the spiritual workings in human life — in their lives as a couple. She is actively contributing to the reunion and has woken to the true love of their meeting and joining. She must bring it back.

You Know Knight?

"Some people will always end up reuniting no matter what happens. You've never left my side in all this time."

They are no longer young and both have had heart breaks — both emotional and physical. They have matching scars. Sometimes lately while working hard towards their reunion she has had sufferings and pain in her physical heart. For this reunion she is actively working towards her renewed health and fitness. She has her doctor onboard with this renewal but her own breath makes sure she must become stronger daily not weaker. She practices deep breathing techniques and is building muscle again.

A failure in her original heart surgery was eventually found by 2022. Long after she suffered disability and struggled to walk around, and catching her breath frequently. No doctor was picking this up. Eventually she asked for checks. They still told her it was all fine. But she collapsed finally with a heart attack. This is when they found the failure and fixed it. She is getting on with her recovery and getting stronger and ready for the amazing reunion now.

This is proof positive that they will both always be protected and healed so they have time left here on Earth for the reunion and atonement to take place. It is in their destinies and can't be changed.

She already knows he loves her more than anyone else in existence. "All these hard times when I'm trying to reach you and you seem so far away — they are not to be worried about or feared. They are not true," she says.

Knight gets closer to her daily. She feels it. She knows it. She is it.

She remains daily in meditation and prayer, creating their life and future for foreverness. This gets both of them into their vortex together daily. Therefore their reunion and joining is inevitable.

If they had really parted then they wouldn't still be in each others' lives. She still has one Golden Ring.

11:11 Signs:

11:11 "The signs have served me well" she says. "I have become aware of 11:11 so many times and received the channelled messages loud and clear." She knows that 11:11 is an angel sign and it means that they are guiding you to know that you are on the right path and that all will be revealed very soon. It is to encourage us to keep going on the path we are on. Yes, we can see it anywhere. On the clock, our phone or a street lighting sign — anywhere at all. Only those who have been made aware of it will notice it.

She awaits the time that Knight will also be wide awake. At this time she is unsure but continues to send him signs and messages. Many times she has become impatient but she knows that she must remain calm and in a state of faith.

In the current time she remembers that she saw in the vortex meeting that there would be a time when she would write more than one book about their lives. They would be published.

She would arrange meetings with her lost Knight and give him a copies of those books. They contain within them, everything he needs to know to continue to awaken and realise who they both are. These books will be available worldwide. Their names being spoken and read by many and this contributes to the process of reunion.

It is a secret key to open doors for them. She can only hope he understands the messages and guides being sent to him. She has to trust in the process. She is fully aware that he is not an avid reader of books so this is a major challenge. At all times The Rings are central to their life path. She now recalls hearing them emphasised when they were in the vortex all those years ago. Suddenly the entire story of The Golden Rings comes into her mind. She knows the Rings as if they are true friends.

The vibrations and energies of The Golden Rings are taking over her mind, body and soul now. Presuming this is also happening to Knight. How can she know? Will he communicate this to her?

The Golden Particles: They swirl and join the rings still, and then encircle Knight and spin further out to where Angel is. Across the distance these swirls connect them together. They are now both entwined to trigger the sleeping spell into new action.

Angel's fragile heart is strengthened by the gold so it will ensure the required time and energy to make things right again for both of them.

She has within her, on good faith from a close friend of them both that he has on two special occasions told this friend that he has "Only loved one special person in this lifetime". And that is Angel. This information has been spoken of before.

His very own spoken words told this evidence. Even once on the occasion of his so-called 'engagement' to another woman. Saying also he will not marry again.

Angel realises this means only that he will not marry another. But fate has it in store for them that they will marry each other again to seal their eternal love.

"As I have said many times before, I can never settle for anyone who is not my Flame." Angel reflects on this statement coming straight from her heart. "All those who are part of a twin flame relationship will know what this means, Knight" she says with total commitment.

He will respond with a deep passionate kiss. "If ever there was The One for me it can be no-one else but you," he will murmur, as they cling deeply and longingly together and not letting go.

In the year 2022 he has also finally kissed the ring. He joked around that he had been hit by a lightning bolt but little did he know he really had been. On the ethereal level. This was an amazing fact that he even agreed to touch it, straight up with no hesitation. He is melting. This sets in motion the future scenes relating to the spell and the pact.

In fact, Angel has another request for him that has huge importance. She will not request this until her second book about Knight is finished. Her request will be for him to travel with her to one of the secret places where they had sworn their undying love for each other so many years ago.

There are many special places that are infused with the spell. They had also clearly left seeds sprinkled there too. She has already been back in time to pick them up.

Here, in this place, she will remind him where they swore these vows. They will stand there once again. Angel had thought, when she was given the secret knowledge and advice of asking him to go on this trip, that he would find a way to refuse. She now knows with certainty that he will agree to go with her. She also knows it will invoke the magic that is urgently needed. After this trip (2023) she knows without any doubts that it will change everything for both of them. They will be together again and he will see the truth once again.

"All this pain," thinks Angel to herself, "it clearly must be worth it." She currently is in an agony of the heart that is threatening to gravely harm her physical heart. Daily she has less and less breath and energy to do physical things. She sometimes lies breathless on her bed or sofa.

Angel also recently found out information about her second husband that sorrowfully tells her the past 28 years she has wasted. The spiritual guides know this is not really true. She has contributed to the welfare of this partner even though it was not always visible. She has done a laborious job.

She sees this as wasted because she can never ever change the outcome — but the time she thinks she wasted by not returning to Knight all those years ago that seem wasted — that cannot be controlled by her. It was a time of learning that was crucial to both Angel and Knight. The spell controlled everything.

It will allow the great burning passion to be released for them in their time left on Earth. Heaven's Grace will gift them extra time on Earth. Although she must leave this current partner as soon as everything has manifested from Knight's point of view and on his side of everything — she still has that, born into her, empathy and hopes he will be ok. She knows that he doesn't really need people, especially intimacy. She can leave it all behind now.

~~~

The Love In You

The Heart In You

...

Became me

CHAPTER 32

Reunion with Fireworks – 2023
– Angel –

*T*he *Memories* will fill our minds with joy and also with the energies that keep us joined. They are tangible 'things' that exist in all directions of time.

The first thing is to replace the 'missing' gold ring. It must be matched as best as humanly possible. Then copy the exact inscription that is inside my ring.

"Oh Knight, my Prince of Hearts, I was a child when we met. We knew nothing of the matched love pact. We recognised each other but ... the fire only smouldered then. I am an adult now with major learning and the fire and passion has matured beyond understanding."

I will speak this to you, Knight, as I came upon the knowledge of who we were and who we now are.

Yes, the awakening of you is imminent now

Star-crossed lovers: Yes, true love smouldered in youth and then got caught up in all the problems put in our way until such time as it appeared to dissipate. This was when we became star-crossed lovers. It seemed to have been watered down. It was not our intention. It was by no means the truth of us. That truth was hidden intentionally but our physical human personalities did not know this. All we saw was a loss and a huge gap in our lives. The breaking was physically painful for us both.

This cannot continue for too long. We will reunite in our current lifetimes. It looks like there's not a lot of time left but no soul ever runs out of time. We have eternity. At the same time we, Knight and Angel, have already pacted our destiny in the paranormal world before we were born. It can't be broken or changed.

Passion and fire in life comes from the Soul Fire within each of us. This is the fire of the soul. If you are part of a Twin Flame relationship you can be assured that the reunion will take place and cannot be missed. No other soul can interfere with how it all plays out. It may look like others are interfering but also this is illusion. Yes, there have been many who have doubted us and our connection.

The places we have been to, our thoughts of each other and sacred symbols we have touched all still carry our energy and the spell has touched them. This will always remain. If we go back to any of these places or touch any of the symbolic items we will instantly be recharged with the pact energy.

Our guides will be instantly by our sides and we will be surrounded by our own Twin Flame love energy.

Two of the first places we will go to from our memories will be Rye back beach and the bush walk at Colbinabbin. These two places have magic in them. First the bush walk at Colbinabbin was where we swore our undying love.

We were teenagers with very little ego or bad energies interfering in our lives.

Rye back beach was one of the last places we were together before our breakup. I 'feel' this energy and know that if we go back there again our magic will start up again. Visiting here is necessary because it will transmute anything sad left there. We can rest assured then that this energy will be gone from us.

In sickness and health, in the good and the bad — I vowed to be with you. I lost sight of even myself for many years — yes, I was lost but now I'm found. Our vows in 1968 are as true to me today as they were then. Let us stay true to them in the now.

I stand by you

Memories are thought of as the past. We must leave the past behind us and live in the now. But … memories are also our learning and the seeds that we left to bring into the now to what we are and what we learnt. If we sprinkle those seeds around us in the present time they will sprout love, good energies and memories to help us on our journey.

Memories are also the sweet thoughts and feelings we had that we need to access right now and bring them into our lives. It is all these years later.

The spell is about to ping! Once it pings then everything falls into place according to our lovers' pact.

We are older now and have many years to catch up on and talk about. Talk! Talk! Talk! You are a good talker and I have pined for this aspect of you. We still have 10 to 20 years together and then eternity. Plenty of time to talk over all our adventures and challenges we had to go through.

I am continuing to grow my hair (you like it longer), I have now organised to have my teeth fixed, my face gets creamed daily, I am still detoxing my body even though a few further heart problems and blood sugars have shown up to be controlled and investigated. The wedding clothes are almost all ready. Just a few items to add to the collection.

I had much work to do on my health and body as the year 2022 started and included quite a few traumas including my infection with the worldwide pandemic virus, fluid collection, untoned body, past open heart surgery fail, a lung disease and a heart attack that required another artery to be repaired. I have been through more tests lately but I am confident that whatever is found will be healed and the time together we have requested from the universe will be granted and manifested for us.

This means I am strong and ready. Knight, you need to be strong and ready also as you have had your fair share of health traumas too.

… Suddenly we were both in the other dimension. Holding hands and looking at past memories. Memories came to life and passed by us.

Each one had soft and sweet feelings that imparted to our minds. We felt dizzy and enlightened. There was a midnight blue aura around everything we looked upon.

"Angel, I never knew how much our love story was central to the healing of an entire universe. Because I now know this, it increases my love for you to be all encompassing. I glow and spiral in our own unique vortex now."

Knight, you now speak your true feelings to me without any reluctance while we are in the vortex. I glowed in this universal light now. Your true love words will always touch the very centre of my soul.

"Knight," I whisper softly. "We are special but only as much as any other souls are special because we are all from the One Soul." A tear of joy quietly pushed its way out from the edge my eye. This specialness is available for all but our own story touches only us while we are living through it.

Then your fingers gently touched my tear and we suddenly spun around in our vortex still clinging together. We landed in the outer dimension with a purple/blue glow coming out from our bodies as a huge aura. There are also silver stars in this aura. We looked down and saw the bright pink glow radiating out from both of our heart chakra areas.

As we then turned towards each other and combined our bodies together, while our individual pink hearts glowing merged into one light that is our one heart.

If we visit together one or more of these past places your mind and soul will awaken. We will temporarily be transported into another dimension while standing together on the Earth where sacred pacts were made. I can hasten and strengthen this energy release if I also wear the jewellery that is sacred to us both. You have touched it before.

That you have also *touched* the ring I am wearing contributes. On the instance of your *touch* the spell of The Golden Rings spins out. This spinout surrounded us both and pulled us into its vortex tightly where we then felt that energy engulf us.

I had fallen into amnesia for many years. I 'forgot' my true love. In my new awakened state I can simply not relate to this time of forgetfulness. I am now fully awake and have access to all the energies that crowd my mind from sacred places and vows we had participated in. I am getting impatient for us to be together as is already destined.

As I've already acknowledged I remarried after leaving you all those years ago but I realise I cannot relate to this second person at all any longer if I ever did. He is causing an imbalance in my energies daily now. We live an unconnected life but together.

I feel the chains as if I am imprisoned. All this because my love has gone. Gone for now but not forgotten and not left behind. This complete love and connection is coming back to both of us.

I see the walk in the Colbinabbin bush now as it was then. I am there with you walking, holding hands. We turn to each other, both hands outstretched towards the other and touching. *Our vows were whispered on the wind. This can never be erased now as the wind has caught the vows and will keep those whispers eternally written.*

… And the wind blows!

This country walk will be accessed as soon as this book is printed and gifted to him. The year 2022 was the year of change and massive endeavours on my part. They will touch you, Knight, but be manifested in 2023. The idea of going there together was imparted to me from spirits.

All of this can last forever. The new Colbinabbin walk in the forest. The inevitable kiss — it can go on and on and never end.

So we will now return to this walk in the bush. Now, it will be in 2023. We will access the power of those vows and catch the wind once again. That whisper on the wind will catapult us again into our vortex, spinning and spinning and catching into our existence, the spell and the pact.

… And the wind blows!

While we are on this country trip I have a few gifts to give you Knight. They are most significant symbolic gifts. You can choose to accept them but if you don't I know for a fact that you will eventually.

There is one gift signifying co-ordinates of a very important place (The Golden Ring), another is inscribed with a place of great importance (our original meeting place) and another is the green FJ Holden. This car is Us and always will be Us.

I'm With You Forever Now
Even into eternity after we leave this planet and this lifetime. I would whither away and die like a

sunflower with no sun if you had not been in my life. It's essential to my very being. As we started off this lifetime as One Soul we cannot be apart.

Now you must come back and renew the golden flower with the sun emanating from your being. We've never been parted in all truth.

We've been through the darkness and learnt more than we possibly knew we needed to know and now it's light.

True Happiness: Everyone wants it. To the point sometimes that they become persuaded they need to steal it from others. The truth is that it is available from inside yourself. You simply must become familiar with the laws of the universe and existence of the soul. It will then be yours without effort because pure joy and happiness belongs to everyone.

Rain Down On Me! The guardian angels have a pre-destined plan to rain down on us two flames, at a certain point in time — the raining will be like stars falling down onto us, into our hearts and minds — all the chosen sweet memories that stir us to the fires.

It started quite some time ago for me. I am touched and brought to tears regularly from this raining of memory stars. I'm not sure about you yet. You still keep much of your emotions hidden from the world. But now is the time for the raining onto you to get stronger and seep into your heart and mind regardless of you trying to push them away.

The Places We Will Go To — Catching the green trams from South City to the City after work. Other times you were waiting for me in the dark after working overtime. You took such great care of me and why was I not letting my passion forcefully flow back in those days. He is also holding back.

If I were back there now in the 1960s I would let my passion run free and wild. I would never listen to society who gave out rules but never followed them. We were fearful fools following rules rather than passion from our own soul. I will always follow my heart now.

That passion and fire will be so huge and burning fiercely that no-one can stop it. There can't be anyone else for either of us. It is already decreed.

We belong to you and me — never let them tell us how to live! Once our reunion has taken place there will be places to go and reignite memories. We will go to Oakleigh, Huntingdale, Springvale and Sorrento. We will revisit all those beautiful times together.

It is written in my heart and I can speak a prophecy for you that we will marry again. Our last wedding and it's forever in this lifetime. It shall be in the same church. It will be in The Church of Emmanuel. We will be fulfilling our destiny.

You burned for me once ... and you will again. I recall that burning very well in my mind and times we were together that it fuelled up. It's a fire that can never be extinguished.

And I burn for you

Once in a lifetime will come a love like ours

Your were the first, and now you will be the last

~~~

We need to recognise the pact
and ever lasting love ...

That our love was always there

It never left ...

We just had to see it

CHAPTER 33

2023: Year of 7 and Time Travel

*T*his year 2023 is 'the' year and they have waited on for an eternity it seems. All the work has been done and lessons learnt up until now. Angel has known that up until 2022 much has been gone through to make the changes and mend the broken hearts. It has been a really tough year. Angel and Knight have both been through those dark times and fallen to rock bottom. They have also risen from the ashes to reach 2023.

They have been hurt, they have been in pain with a lot of crying. Year 2023 is the key to the heavenly number 7. "This is when I can stop time and the constant wheel we are all in." says Angel out loud.

"If I change time and fate by my action to love, reunite and heal others and myself then it changes the fate of many," she thinks with amazement. This time change spreads out to a wide distance — just like the beat of the butterfly's wings can trigger a chain reaction millions of miles away.

People say you have to see it to believe it …
But … It is the other way around:

You have to believe it to see it — always.

People who belong together — but are apart will definitely be together again soon, now and forever. "I will see you in the summer. We will soak up the warmth of the sun while gazing with passion into each other's eyes and melting into each other's arms. Forever …"

"There was a once upon a time era — so good — so filled with love, that you can never let it go." Angel murmurs. We met in the spring — then spring became the summer. It was that summer of never ending love. Never let go … But this time we meet in the winter but summer is on its way soon.

She is also aware that the year 2023 is 'The Year' when everything manifests on the Earth plane — for them — and for many others. We will actually physically see the results.

No-one else knows that this special year involves some time travel that Angel herself has learnt about and is facilitating for both the Twin Flames and all those connected to them in any way, shape or form. All those others will also feel that pull of time change.

She already has witnessed the start of changes in the lives of their four children.

This is the time when she can stop time and we will be released from the constant wheel of time we are all in.

Angel says to herself: "If I change time and fate by my actions to love, reunite and heal others and myself, then it changes the fate and destiny of many, many people around us and connected to us in even the slightest way."

It would be like the 'butterfly effect' mentioned before. This butterfly effect can be explained in simple terms. It is the idea that small changes can have major effects on complex systems seemingly unconnected to the butterfly.

You see the secret is that all the time and fate changes took place mostly before 2022 and will be culminating in 2023. This was a traumatic and chaotic year for this reason.

By the time 2023 comes, everything has changed. Destinies have altered, as they all can when you put your mind to work on making changes. Time works differently. 2023 – that magic number (7) brings its production of events that resolve past problems. Love blooms like a flower. It needs to be nurtured.

If Angel just goes to a place from the past where the twin flames had been together in love and if she picks up even just a pebble or a leaf and takes it with her to another place. It's a place of Now. Then that changes the rest of the world around them and its happenings. She understands that now. She has that mission to go on. Now as soon as everything is ready. She will make those collections in every place.

Right throughout our time together here, as we made memories filled with love and joy we dropped seeds along the way. They are everywhere. Angel can stop time now and go back and pick the seeds up. She has mastered time travel, she goes back, picks up all the seeds and brings them back to Now in her pocket.

She discovered previously about the seeds from the past and how those sprouting flowers spread mystic timeline pollen into the minds and aura of the Twin Flames. This ignites in them the feelings and the memories.

May we leave the rest of the world behind? There is only us. We will leave the naysayers and the foolish behind us and we will live without any thought of them.

"Bruce, you just have to look at your life right now and decide that it is not you and that only you and me can be 'you'. We need no-one else. We are 'you and me'. We are our children. We are our grand children."

"The world should let us be. We decide that we are One. We belong to you and me and no other single person existing decides that for us."

Today Angel has picked up first the tarot card called The Lovers. Its meaning is connected to all that she is doing right now. Her fate and destiny are sealed in this card and because of her connection to Knight then his is also sealed in this choice.

~~~

It is our challenge to wake up

To realise where our lost true love went

...

To recognise those unreal ogres in our lives

CHAPTER 34

The Healing Intention: 1963-2023

*L*ove is a Healing Intention. Many of us agree to Twin Flame incarnations to contribute to the Healing Intention of Love in the universe. We contribute for the sake of all, including the entire Earth, not just ourselves.

The Golden Rings saga that is them, will forever be a contribution to mankind. In doing this their own love will prosper. This story goes down in universal history and is held in the Akashic Records forever. Anyone can access the story for themselves and for their own advancement. Only on the spiritual level.

It is recognised that when souls commit to this kind of Earth life they are not just healing themselves and close family but they can easily extend it to surround the entire world.

The world is on a collision course to heal and change to a place of love and care, beauty and peace. Those who are here right now and are from the dark side, who are harming humans, creatures and the Eco system — seem blindly to do these things unaware they are actually harming themselves. They are ignorant to the ways of truth and nature.

Situations like the souls of Twin Flame birthings go through all sorts of dark places after they meet in love but they are armed with the universal spell and guardian support to find their way back even stronger and releasing even more love. This love they release when they reunite can be directed wherever they desire it to be.

Both when they are together and apart, they will go through many challenges. The first set of challenges will try their relationship while they are still together. Many things will then contribute to them splitting. Something neither could ever have imagined at the start of their love together here.

"Dear Knight" says Angel, as she is feeling great blocks missing from their lives. "I can't believe there have been so many years that I've missed out on in your life and our life."

"I want to know everything about the years of your life we both missed. I know much of our stories we will tell each other will contain deep dark bad times we both went through. But the sharing and the telling will help to join us and heal us."

"It will be painful but let's do it. Light will be shone on our pain."

They will only spend a few nights talking about this. It can't be allowed to taint their new life together by talking of the darknesses far into their future. This talking will heal their darkness. Forever after that they only talk of love each day and what they are doing for each other from now on.

They can talk all night if they wish to. No-one can interfere because it's their lives. "We are us and us only, alongside our descending family who are also part of us."

Beginning their reunion, this talking all night will be their focus. They won't be able to stop the flow of it. The words and experiences will pour from them.

After all, it's only 30 years out of forever that they missed each other and were apart. That is virtually nothing in the whole scheme of the infinite universe of their Twin Flame lives. Just a grain of sand.

Those other partners Knight and Angel met, stayed with, or married in those long in-between years are simply challenges. Angel had met someone she thought was saving her from her deep loss of Knight. But ... the angels and guides had sent her a really huge challenge. She was completely unaware from the start. It is soon that she finds various problems with this partner. He is awkward and has a different way of thinking and being in the world to her and unlike anyone she so far ever met.

At first, many times did Knight try to bring her back but that powerful spell that tells the universe that they must spend long years apart to learn unconditional love interferes with her mind and thinking. That spell, that pact, it is so powerful they can feel the pull and cannot resist its strength.

In the present time, now that she has awakened she can look back and see all the errors in her thinking and how, if that had been in the now time, she would never make those mistakes of judgement.

She would never leave him and she would have worked to bring back their love and connection before she left. But that is only her current, in the Now, thinking because she has been through the dark places and she has learnt about true love — and all of that was necessary in the plan.

"Our Close Encounter: 2022 — Angel—"

I see you today and as I sit next to you — I feel that pull of the spell — I feel that attraction that is telling me to wrap my arms around you and take you home right now to our place.

"Yes, to our place. We have a place in our destiny where there is just you and me. We know we will be there no matter what it takes and how long it takes," says Angel. That is up to both of us and the timings in which both or either of us wake up fully and realise. That is the time and place where our own family also reunites in the love they were born into but have lost sight of over these many years. I sometimes look at you, I see you, sometimes you look sad. I can't allow you to cry, I can't allow you ever to be sad or alone. This can never be. It is me who will dry your eyes.

It's my job now to love you, bring you only joy every single day. All that love and joy we both missed out on. When I think about it now it seems it was for no reason. There is absolutely no reason why we didn't merge into one and stay that way all our lives.

"The only real reason was our pact and the spell we chose to be under. We were chosen and we agreed to all the challenges. We both wanted to be brave. We desired the learning from The University of the Universe" Angel muses.

Destiny is a pull. You can feel it if you are sensitive enough. Unless you are very strong and determined then you are useless to resist it. It's not possible for most people.

When your destiny or karma is leading you somewhere or on a path then go with it. If it's a karmic thing you wish to avoid you must make atonement first to avoid it.

~~~

My Love Knows No Bounds

...

I Love You To Infinity

...

CHAPTER 35

The Rings Continue: 1980+

*T*he Rings were still sending energies and guidance from their differing places of rest. The lost ring pulsating out waves of light prompted the Twin Flames to drop all their current illusions and return to each other. Only then would a new ring and new life be generated in the world. The female ring that now stood waiting on the right hand of Angel received these waves of messages.

Soon the new replacement gold ring would be purchased and worn by Knight. The engraving would be emulated and instantly all would be well in their ongoing lives. The reunion is almost complete.

The Rings have survived, as has their power. Prophecies and spells would be in aligrment once again. Nothing can lessen the power and energy sent out by the missing ring at the muddy bottom of the lake in Goughs Bay, Eildon. This location is now recorded forever into infinity. It has great meaning.

The Twin Flames have gone through their challenges that included a split and reunion and new life. New life is the new ring matching the original.

A new Jeweller has already been found. He must be right for the job. Not many make this exact shape and gold carat ring anymore.

There is really only one huge great boulder in the way of their reunion happening right now. Sometimes it intimidates Angel greatly. But the truth is that it may only be a tiny small pebble or grain of sand that is really in the way. Life is all about how you perceive things.

So therefore if she chooses to see only a tiny grain of sand that can be brushed aside — that means there is no longer anything at all in their way. Therefore they will meet and make music.

There is also the fact that at a recent family event she sat very close to him at a table and she shone the golden ring (original ring) she was wearing directly at him. She made sure to mentally send golden particles from the spell of the ring into and surrounding his heart, his mind and his entire being.

These particles spun around and around, then also surrounded her own heart, mind and being. This caused all those spellbound golden particles to surround them both together. She concentrated as if in a meditative state all this time.

She allowed this occur for a number of minutes — enough to spark the spell and pact into action.

She was also very much made aware that he was lonely. He is with another partner and so is Angel. But they are both very lonely. Those relationships both lack true love and connection for them.

When will they wake up together and run to each other?

~~~

I love you more than the world

Always Have

Always Will!

...

If you had not been born
Then neither would I have been

...

As Our Souls and Connections
go forever into eternity together!

...

CHAPTER 36

Angel's Heart – 2020-2022

*A*ngel's *heart was* broken when they lost sight of each other all those years ago. She had her physical heart mended in hospital just as he had his mended about 12 years ago. His was the first sign of their broken hearts in the physical world. When hers broke years later after much strain, then it was obvious to those who could understand on the next level — that those two hearts were one.

They promised. They promised each other and gave assurances many years ago. With the spells and pacts surrounding them and the power of The Golden Rings, it means they are supported to keep all promises forever. They are not only supported but pacted by their promises.

These are promises that can never even be contemplated to be broken. It can't happen. While it may seem that they were broken they were only ever at times bent slightly. Any promise broken was an illusion. Human promises are broken constantly but not those that are pacted.

They are only broken truly when they can't be mended and brought back to life again. It's mostly within twin flame relationships that have the splits and reunions that you will find promises cannot be broken. It's not possible. With atonement and reunion they are mended again. Absolutely everything can be mended or fixed.

The word Promise either spoken or written has major vibrations of energy that are sacred to all those who use it or speak it. Those people whose promises were never kept never really connected to the word. They went through their lives and completely forgot the word and its meaning.

Twin Flames never forget or disregard their promises. Sometimes it just may look like they have for the sake of their path in life. When Angel ran away for a while it certainly seemed she had forgotten the Promises. This was meant to be or the Split of the Flames could not have happened. Even she was fooled into forgetting the Promises. But they stayed deep within her heart. Knight thought she had broken her promises too. He had even, of course, broken promises himself but never noticed.

Angel actually realised suddenly that the past 30 years were illusions. Even in 2019 way before 2020, she 'knew'. Knight also lived his own illusions all this time. They can all be dissolved. Like Knight, Angel's heart has been mended more than once. She is currently undergoing more and more tests because even after her recent mending in hospital, she felt clean and well for a few weeks, but then her symptoms returned.

This can be put down to her losing a bit of faith, although she has always tried to keep with the faith of the pact. She has tried her best to not worry but worry is within her healing, her mending heart and mind towards others. She was made that way.

The one thing they should never be afraid of is 'Starting Over Again'. They would not be starting from scratch (with absolutely no knowledge or experience). But they would be starting from extensive experience. They will know all the pitfalls because they've already fallen into them before and never will again.

All this time when they thought they were lost, they now know it was a feeling of their hearts and souls searching for each other for a seemingly eternity of time. But the time has already been decided. The time of change is at hand.

~~~

…

I've never known love like ours

…

Knowing you're with me
Now and Forever
Makes everything ok

… Bruce

CHAPTER 37

Her Dreams: 2021-2023

*T*he first of her reality dreams came to Angel in this timeline. In all of her years on Earth she has rarely had dreams about actual people in her life. They were not ever about her lover. In this timeline 2021-22 she has now had at least four dreams of Knight. They are reality dreams, not in a weird dreamscape like dreams usually are.

The first one takes her into his townhouse. She was in the lounge room. It was so real, not like dreams that are fragmented and unreal looking. It was just like dreams she has sometimes had before that were actual experiences on the astral level. It showed Angel she belonged there or anywhere that he resided.

We didn't just accidentally *find each other*

We were inside each other all along

Dreams that feel like reality and have shown up recently indicate that they are predictive. Your thoughts and your creations for your life can show up in very reality-like dreams. You would not be in a typical 'dream-like' state of unreality with warped scenes.

Another dream was an actual dream playing out her thoughts and fears. To manifest the good these thoughts must be eliminated and then those dreams would not come. All the same, this dream could still be predictive. It shows her that she still harbours fears and the manifestation of Twin Flame Reunion must only be based on the good vibrations and matching vortex.

'This Dream' of fears: She felt like crying all day that day again. She fell into a deep sleep or a kind of unconsciousness once again.

She woke suddenly at 2.30am. It was from a nightmare again. 'She was in a prison where all those that were there and wished to escape had to hide in some kind of camouflage. Everything looked like blue icing on a cake and all had to blend into it. If they were seen something bad would happen.' This dream was a culmination of her many fears over the years and the fact that whenever she lost faith she felt trapped or imprisoned.

Fortunately, she woke with a sudden start. All at once she was aware that she had escaped. She felt it all for the next day. But above all else, she was now aware that she would be escaping very soon. These good vibe thoughts have to be kept close to the heart so that they can manifest on the physical world level.

She now knows that she can create these dreams of him. She can dream of reality with both of them together. All she has to do now is meditate deeply, just before sleep, on what she wants her dream to be for any given night and that creates it deep in her subconscious to a reality dream.

She also later dreamt they were out in public together for the first time. There were people all around them that knew them.

He came to her and kissed her while others noticed this. They all asked if they were together again. This dream within it created thoughts of 'oh we've now let everyone know'.

This dream signalled how they would be demonstrating their reunion to all those that knew them well.

~~~

I would never have

existed without you Knight

...

And clearly you would never have

existed without me

...

CHAPTER 38

The Now: 2022-2023
– Angel –

I am finally confident in knowing who I am. I have the learning of a lifetime within me. You are me and I am you. We are One, as was preordained in the pact of our destiny together here on Earth. It was also in the spell of The Golden Rings. It is all coming together in the Now.

The separations and the irrelevant relationships are done and their memories are already fading away into the far distance of time. Time, which we no longer have to live within. There is a whole lot of dancing and celebrations to be going through — the laughter and the joy. There is 'a wedding of all weddings' to be planned. Most of those plans are within my psyche and have been there all along.

All of the relatives and friends who are truly sacred friends will be there. They will laugh — they will also lose their sorrows in this joy. Some will not control their laughter because it has been held inside far too long. Their own personal pain, sadness and dark times will also be obliterated in the light. We are connected far and beyond the end of this life. There were errors along the way such as:

We didn't touch each other enough

Neither emotionally; nor physically

We just did not know then. Dear God, please give us that chance to do it right now. Right now — this lifetime. Give us many years left on Earth to touch, not only each other, but those around us.

Throw us the crumbs of life and we vow to make them into the pearls. It is all part of our destined lifetime here and now. Give us the patience and calmness of mind to wait for it all to fall into place. There are decreed timelines, so waiting is required.

"Knight," I cry out, "you need to recognise that no matter who you are with and whether you imagine that is your love life, there is never anyone else on this planet who is matched to you but me."

We are matched for everything. Our hearts have been broken and our chests sawn open, and the scars of this and the scars of our lives match perfectly.

It is done!

No matter who you are with, if it is not me, then it's all wrong and so is your life until you are fully awake to our pact and the spell. You will awaken. This is certain. You can't change destiny or your fate if it is coming from a pact or fight any spiritual spell. We are choosing our own lives, all of us. Even inactivity is choosing your life. If you do nothing you are still choosing and making a life choice.

Would I Ever Shy Away? Would I shy away from directly speaking to and asking Knight 'to come right back'? Why should I waver on this now?

The spell doesn't allow for that. I must be brave and push myself forward. This is why the spell exists and also why I exist — for the learning and for making me stronger. If I desire the love and happiness we were both born for, then I must go forward to make my requests and desires known.

Don't Worry Knight! I am saving you as you are saving me. Not too long to wait now. Hang in there!

Don't worry darling! I'm coming for you. Don't worry darling! No-one else will do.

We are both living lives deep in depression a lot of the time. It's temporary and it's because the reunion and manifesting is about to appear right in front of us.

This type of unstable energy that is burning and stirring and about to manifest can sometimes have unsettling effects on the participants.

We can feel the pressure in the air around us and the wondering in our minds of when and where all this amazing life will come to be. We know and feel its pressing presence but it's not visible yet. Daily now it pushes onto us to guide and influence us.

He feels it more than I do because a lot of the time he lives alone. Yes, he has a new partner who seems to care for him. But it's not in the way he desires or requires. He is, after-all, a Twin Flame and a Scorpio. He can only live his love life completely, not half and half.

Once the manifesting is complete and I have moved in with him and all our plans and ceremonies have come about we will never leave each others' sides ever again. Not even in any part of eternity. Our love goes far and beyond into infinity. Nothing that exists in the universe can stop it or contain it ever. It has a life of its own.

This depression also is in both of us because of our split and long years without each other. To this day I find it an unbelievably empty time.

We do have to make the effort to get into the higher energies of our combined vortex so that everything manifests in the physical. That will happen naturally as soon as I have completed my work. All that has to happen is the rejoining. We must make up our minds as lovers.

Anniversaries: We will celebrate monthly anniversaries from that reunion day onwards. This is making up for all the years we missed.

It is also because the rest of our life together is now shorter. After our wedding we change it to monthly from that date. Life can be beautiful — if you make it beautiful!

Angel is Once Again a Virgin

This wedding is set so much the same, similar and the very energies of the first but with true hindsight so that no mistakes are made this time around. There is also the essential newness in this ceremony.

My dress pure white and my heart beating strong … Just like 1968. White silk and made by a dressmaker to fit me exactly as I will be strong and fit again by that time. Knight is a dream in his chosen suit. Different this time. It is a white jacket with possibly a maroon bow tie. There will be many photographs on this day and a film to show our family. Once again I do my best to manipulate time travel to bring everything here to us in the Now. "Oh Knight, if you don't come back, touch my neck and brush my hair — what will I do without you?"

We will live on forever now, after this day it will never end. So much joy would Knight already have if he could only know and believe the truth.

… and the wind blows

True love stories never have endings

~~~

Never Let Me Go

...

*Now That I Have
Found You Again*

...

I Will Never Let Go Again

EPILOGUE

Knight now has the opportunity to regain the love of his life. He is on the precipice of either awakening or remaining asleep. Him being open to remembering his vows before birth is now vital to his wellbeing.

The Golden Rings have done their job as has the Jeweller and the spirit guides. All of them work with the spell created in the far dimensions. Spell incantations never ever fail. How can they fail? But subjects to spells can remain closed off and prevent the spell from spinning around in their minds for quite some time. The spell will win out in the end. There is purely no doubt about that. Angel can rest assured of that. Knight's personal guides now remain around him to help to awaken him. Destiny relies on this process working on him.

All will still not be lost if he does not awaken in this lifetime. Life has moved on for both the Twin Flames and they are now growing older. They can still have 5 or ten years together to let their passions loose and reignite what they had as mere children. Their love remained innocent and naive all those years. Only now does Angel see how they never let their passionate fire loose. They never let go.

What they have learnt in the Twin Flame split and breakup is that their original love was never extinguished. They can now see how their real passions were held down and then they eventually broke because of this.

The Split was organised on high just for the very reason of their learning, forgiving and the coming of the reuniting. They could then 'Let Go' and live the passions gifted to them. The spell itself worked on their minds driving them apart against their original will. It was always and ever for their own good and learning although it didn't seem like that.

Angel has the learning in her heart and soul now. She knows. She feels and has experienced all their former connections and passions. She knows that passion was never 'let loose'. She feels the wanting for this to occur. It's an absolute desire. She wants Knight to feel it and experience it also. She fully longs for him to experience true and absolute love here on the Earth plane with her.

"I owe you this Knight," she vows. "The real fire passions are ready and waiting to come to the surface now." She knows and feels this every single day. She does not need to lament because they owe this to each other. They both must meet equally on this plane. They both were innocent and withholding. They can now break free and live their utmost life together. It was almost a virtual reality situation. They needed to wake up. That's all — nothing else is required.

This book is the Prequel to the author's book 'Twin Flame Reunion' in which the play of Knight's and Angel's twin flame experience on Earth is told. The next book, the sequel, 'Twin Flames United' will reveal the outcome of their endeavours and challenges in this incarnation.

The third book completes the 'Twin Flame Saga'. It's up to the reader to conclude whether Angel and Knight are actual people or fiction.

"My dear Knight (who is also Bruce) please choose the best for you and the best for me."

"This is the chance for us. This was the sacred spell created with just us in mind."

"We must let our other partners go now. They must fade to dust. They have always only ever been soul mates for the purpose of us reuniting."

She has known this for a very long time. She has already told her current partner they are not suited as true loves and that they will inevitably part in this lifetime. He knows that, if he was truly listening. But he continues to act and live out his life as if this will never actually happen.

All Knight needs to do now is to tell his current partner the true story. Tell her how things will really be and that they must now make arrangements to part their ways. It's not that hard for him as he and his current partner never really committed to each other. In that, they don't live together, they don't combine their possessions or finances and their families are now mostly kept apart.

All that's needed here is a truthful and meaningful conversation and a decision not to go out or see each other again. It's quite simple but he may find it hard to do. Courage is needed.

For Angel it's not so simple, but at the same time she has been planning it for years. She has the process in her mind and just needs to execute it swiftly. The papers are ready for the legal and final break for her. Her current partner knows very well he is not the love of her life. He appears not to care and is a closed-in personality. This personality is what drove her to desperation many times in their marriage. Wasted years when she and Knight could have been together creating the passionate life they were born for.

To Knight, now, her words ring out:
"Choose Love at its highest and passion at its hottest right now in the remainder of our life-time here."

"You are my everything — no-one is ever going to Love You like I do. It's not even possible. We will be One, Always and Ever."

What to do if the spell hasn't pinged on Knight yet? That really isn't in Angel's life plan of manifesting.

But ... IF ... Then perhaps read the third book in the series to find out what she would do.

They will always be back together. There's no way not to be ... but ... if it's not very soon, like this lifetime then will Angel have to make a new plan?

She has always known it should be this lifetime but maybe it can be later rather than sooner. It all depends on whether Knight has allowed himself to be vulnerable to the spell as well as the awakening.

In the meantime can she continue to live the way she is? With someone who means nothing and often goes out of his way to make many days intolerable and miserable for her? Her tears flow. She will now wait forever Knight. No matter what it takes. Forever goes far and beyond this lifetime for both of them.

She now knows why she didn't make the move during the car show days when it seemed very possible from his point of view. It is because the spell had not yet spun its stories in Angel's mind for the books yet. The books were always crucial to the spell.

If We Live To Infinity – And We Love For Eternity Then what is destiny? What is our fate? We can't reach our destiny or even our fate, because we still go on and on after that. All people should rethink their ideas of what destiny or fate really is and that it is not really achievable in the way they think it is.

People have the complete wrong concept of reality and infinity. Reaching our fate or our destiny conveys a meaning to many that you have somehow come to the end of your journey. This is absolutely false and fools many people.

There is no end. These two words (fate and destiny) are only meaning that they are the stepping stones to achieve and then move on and learn more.

Throughout, the main body of this book and the tale is a paranormal love story novel but the entire rest is autobiographical.

Therefore this is my given clue as to the reality of this book. The 'fairytale style' parts are exact metaphors to the reality of those very real Twin Flames and their own actual experiences.

You can only discover if their 'Reunion' became a reality by reading the final book in the set of 3. The book called 'Twin Flames United' is the sequel to 'Twin Flame Reunion'.

If you are looking for the finale to know if everything works with the spell then it will be available late 2023 or early 2024.

~~~

Our Soul is One

Twin Flames Forever

...

We will return in every Lifetime

...

About the Author

Coral Y. Cross started her education in the writing field at art school, studying art history and writing short stories. Her intention was always to publish eventually. But in the mean time she studied photography, graphic design and illustration. She then worked for many years in the editorial section of magazines and newspapers and eventually as an advertising designer. Coral Y. Cross has also worked in the healing and spiritual areas for many years. She is qualified in Kahuna Massage/Healing, Bodywork, and Pranic (energy) Healing. She has also studied the teachings of forgiveness, atonement, law of attraction and manifesting.

She has used the base of this healing education and qualifications to go deep and evolve spiritually to the point where she recognised her gift to access intuitive information for healing and writing. She uses her gift extensively in her writing. This gift is usually spontaneous.

She has self published three other books. The sequel to this book and 2 others dealing with healing chronic pain and illness which you can find at Amazon books and other online stores or at www.choose-to-heal.com.au

Books by this author:
'The Golden Rings'
'Twin Flame Reunion'
'Heal Chronic Pain & Disease'
'Healing Practices'